P9-CQK-020

"Can I help?"

Hadn't she helped enough?

"No." Wyatt walked away because it was a lot easier than staying there to answer more of her questions. He knew it probably seemed rude, but she didn't have a clue.

Rachel didn't know that he was rebuilding his family and that it took every bit of energy he had. Everything he had went to his girls, into making them smile and making their lives stable.

As he walked into the barn, he glanced back. Rachel leaned to talk to Kat. Curls fell forward, framing her face, but a hand came up to push her hair back. She smiled and leaned to kiss his daughter on the cheek.

He walked into the shadowy interior of the barn and flipped on a light. He breathed in the familiar scents. Cows, horses, hay and leather. He could deal with this. He couldn't deal with a beautiful woman who seemed to love his girls as much as he did.

Books by Brenda Minton

Love Inspired

Trusting Him
His Little Cowgirl
A Cowboy's Heart
The Cowboy Next Door
Rekindled Hearts
Blessings of the Season
  "The Christmas Letter"
Jenna's Cowboy Hero
The Cowboy's Courtship
The Cowboy's Sweetheart
Thanksgiving Groom
The Cowboy's Family

BRENDA MINTON

started creating stories to entertain herself during hour-long rides on the school bus. In high school she wrote romance novels to entertain her friends. The dream grew and so did her aspirations to become an author. She started with notebooks, handwritten manuscripts and characters that refused to go away until their stories were told. Eventually she put away the pen and paper and got down to business with the computer. The journey took a few years, with some encouragement and rejection along the way—as well as a lot of stubbornness on her part. In 2006 her dream to write for the Steeple Hill Love Inspired line came true. Brenda lives in the rural Ozarks with her husband, three kids and an abundance of cats and dogs. She enjoys a chaotic life that she wouldn't trade for anything—except, on occasion, a beach house in Texas. You can stop by and visit at her website, www.brendaminton.net.

The Cowboy's Family
Brenda Minton

Steeple
Hill®

Published by Steeple Hill Books™

If you purchased this book without a cover you should be aware
that this book is stolen property. It was reported as "unsold and
destroyed" to the publisher, and neither the author nor the
publisher has received any payment for this "stripped book."

STEEPLE HILL BOOKS

Steeple
Hill®

Recycling programs
for this product may
not exist in your area.

ISBN-13: 978-0-373-81523-4

THE COWBOY'S FAMILY

Copyright © 2011 by Brenda Minton

All rights reserved. Except for use in any review, the reproduction
or utilization of this work in whole or in part in any form by any
electronic, mechanical or other means, now known or hereafter
invented, including xerography, photocopying and recording, or in
any information storage or retrieval system, is forbidden without
the written permission of the editorial office, Steeple Hill Books,
233 Broadway, New York, NY 10279 U.S.A.

This is a work of fiction. Names, characters, places and incidents are
either the product of the author's imagination or are used fictitiously, and
any resemblance to actual persons, living or dead, business establishments,
events or locales is entirely coincidental.

This edition published by arrangement with Steeple Hill Books.

® and TM are trademarks of Steeple Hill Books, used under license.
Trademarks indicated with ® are registered in the United States Patent
and Trademark Office, the Canadian Trade Marks Office and in other
countries.

www.SteepleHill.com

Printed in U.S.A.

Thou hast turned for me my mourning into dancing:
Thou hast put off my sackcloth,
and girded me with gladness.
—*Psalms* 30:11

To my readers.

And especially to Julie, for your prayers,
your thoughtfulness and your insight.

To Stephanie Newton, for those
last minute critiques!

Chapter One

Why had she thought this was a good idea, cleaning house for Wyatt Johnson? Rachel Waters cut the engine to her car and stared up at the big, brick home that Wyatt had built over the winter. She pushed her sunglasses to the top of her head as she mulled the reasons for being here. First of all, she'd agreed to this as a favor to Ryder and Andie. Second, she struggled with the word *no*.

There were plenty of reasons not to be here. She didn't need the money. She didn't need the headache.

She especially didn't need the heartache.

And Wyatt Johnson had heartache written all over his too-handsome face. Heartache was etched into his eyes. It was the whisper of a smile on his lips. It hovered over his lean features when he picked up his girls from the church nursery, hugging them but saying little to her or the other nursery workers.

So what had she gone and done? As if she didn't have enough to occupy her time, Rachel had agreed when Ryder Johnson asked her to clean the house his brother Wyatt had built on land across the road from the original Johnson ranch house, the house Ryder and his wife Andie now called home.

Rachel eyed the brick, French country-style home. The windows were wide, the porch was brick and stone. The landscaping was professionally done, but the flowers were being choked out by weeds.

It was a far cry from the parsonage she'd shared with her parents for the last year; since her dad took the job as pastor of the Dawson Community Church. Their little house could fit into this one five times. But the parsonage was immaculate. If her father could get hold of these gardens, he could do wonders with the place.

Oh, well, she couldn't put it off forever. She hopped out of her car. A border collie bounded toward her, tail wagging. The animal, black-and-white coat clean and brushed, rolled over at her feet. Rachel leaned to pet the dog's belly.

"So, at least you get some attention, huh, girl?"

That wasn't fair. Wyatt tried, she was sure he

tried. But his girls often came to church with ragged little braids and mismatched clothes. Not that the girls seemed to mind. They smiled and hugged him, and then waited for him to pick them up again.

Rachel cast a critical gaze over the lawn and the house. The barns and fences surrounding the place were well-kept. The horses grazing in the fields gleamed in the early spring sunshine. She'd spent a lifetime dreaming of a place like this.

She walked up the patio steps and knocked on the back door. She stood there for a long time, looking out over the fields, talking aimlessly to the dog. She knocked again. From inside she heard children talking and the drone of the television.

She knocked a third time.

Finally footsteps headed her way and a male voice said something about the television show they were watching. She stepped back and the door opened. Wyatt Johnson stared at her, his dark hair longish. His brown eyes with flecks of dark green were fringed with long lashes. Gorgeous eyes and a gorgeous man. She nearly groaned. He stared at her and then looked down. Two little heads peeked out at her. Molly, age three, and Kat, age two. Molly had told her that she'd be turning four in a few of weeks.

"Can I help you?" Wyatt didn't move, didn't

invite her in. He just stared, as if he didn't have a clue who she was. Six months he'd been home. Six months she'd held his girls and read them stories. Sundays had flown by and each week he'd signed the girls in, signed them out and she'd asked how he was doing.

She was the invisible Rachel Waters. He was probably trying to decide where he knew her from.

"I'm here to clean," she explained, and she managed to smile.

"Clean?"

She held up the bucket she'd taken from her car and the tub of cleaning supplies. "Clean your house. Ryder hired me."

"He didn't say anything to me."

"No, he probably didn't. Surprise!" She smiled at the girls. They giggled. At least they thought she was funny.

Kat, hands pudgy, her smile sweet, pushed against Wyatt and slipped outside. Rachel wasn't invisible to Kat. Or to Molly.

"We have crayons."

"That's wonderful, Kat. Are you coloring a picture?"

Kat nodded. "For Mommy. Daddy said we could mail it to heaven."

"That's a lovely idea." That was the heartache in

his eyes. Rachel didn't look up because she didn't want to see his pain. His story was his, private, that's how he'd kept it. She understood. She had her own stories.

Molly remained behind Wyatt, but she moved a little and peeked out from behind his legs. "I like coloring flowers."

"I think flowers are one of my favorite things, Molly. It's April, we'll have lots of flowers blooming very soon."

Rachel glanced up. Wyatt hadn't moved. He just stared for a long minute and then he shook his head and let out a long sigh. It sounded a lot like someone giving up. It didn't seem as if he'd changed his mind about her, though, because he didn't move an inch.

"I don't think we need help with the house."

Rachel peeked past him and her nose wrinkled. "I disagree."

He glanced back over his shoulder and shrugged. "It isn't that bad."

"It is bad." Molly waved a hand in front of her nose. "It's smelly bad. That's what Uncle Ryder said when he came home last week from the rodeo circus."

"Circuit." Wyatt corrected and then his gaze was back on Rachel. "I don't need help with the house."

He leaned against the door frame, faded jeans, bare feet and a T-shirt. She took a step back, putting herself out of his personal space and back into her own.

"Ryder already paid me." And she didn't like backing down. "I have a few hours free today, no time tomorrow. I'm not going to take his money and not do the job."

"Ryder should have checked with me. The girls and I were about to clean."

"After Daddy traces our hands and then does bank stuff." Molly supplied the information with all the innocence of an almost-four-year-old.

"Sounds like fun." Rachel stood on the porch, sun beating down on her back. Wyatt continued to stare and she felt fifteen and overweight. She wasn't, but that look took her back about fifteen years to a place in her life that she really didn't want to return to.

"Honestly, Rachel, we don't need a house-keeper."

"Sorry." She smiled and took a step forward. Ryder and Andie had warned her that he'd be stubborn about this.

"Yeah, I'm sure."

"So, I can come in?" Rachel glanced at her watch. She really didn't have all day.

Wyatt, tall and cowboy lean, shrugged and

stepped back. He waved her in and she was pretty sorry she'd ever agreed to do this. Dishes covered the counters and the sink overflowed. Toys were scattered across a floor that hadn't seen a mop in, well, it looked like a long time.

"I guess it's a mess." Wyatt smiled a little and scooped up Kat to settle her on his shoulders. "We haven't really paid much attention."

She wanted to ask how he could not pay attention but that insult piled up on top of a dozen other things she wanted to say to him. His daughters were still in their pajamas and he hadn't shaved in days. This wasn't a life; this was hiding from life.

Wyatt had been home for more than six months and from what she'd seen, he hadn't done a thing to step back into life here, other than church on Sundays and meals at the Mad Cow. Oh, and he'd bought horses. He always had his girls in tow, though. She had to give him credit for that.

He couldn't match an outfit for anything, but he loved Molly and Kat.

So this was how his brother planned on pushing him back into the dating world. She was probably clueless and really thought this was about cleaning the house. Wyatt planned a few choice words for Ryder as Rachel Waters stepped away from him and leaned to talk to Kat, dusting his daughter's hands off in the process. The back of Rachel's shirt came up a little and he couldn't look away.

He must have made a sound because she straightened and shifted her shirt back into place. Her face was a little pink and she glanced away from him as she pulled her dark, curly hair into a ponytail. She continued to ignore him and he couldn't stop thinking about a butterfly tattoo at the waist of her jeans. Did the church nursery worker have secrets?

A little late he remembered to be resentful. His younger brother had a habit of pushing his way into people's lives and shoving his ideas off on them. Rachel cleaning the house was Ryder's idea.

Wyatt kept his own ideas to himself, the way he'd been doing for the last few months. He didn't have time or energy to worry about Rachel or what Ryder was up to.

"I guess if you're here to clean, have at it." He nodded in the direction of the kitchen. He'd put a lot of thought into building this house. Granite countertops, stainless steel appliances and tile floors. It should have gleamed. Instead it looked like a bunch of teenagers had ransacked the place.

He hadn't meant to reminisce, but he remembered his parents' kitchen after it had been ransacked by Wyatt, Ryder and their friends. He and Ryder hadn't been easy to raise. Not that their parents had done a lot of raising; more like they'd just turned them loose and told them to do whatever, as long as they didn't land in jail.

Rachel looked around the kitchen, her mouth open a little. Yeah, it was pretty bad. He didn't have time to do everything. The girls came first, then the farm, then business. Last, and probably least, the house.

"Need anything?" he asked, turning his attention back to Rachel Waters.

"No, thanks. If you don't mind, I'll get started." She smiled, a wide smile that settled in dark brown eyes.

"I don't mind. I'll be in the office with the girls. Don't worry about upstairs."

"Seriously? Wyatt, your brother paid me a lot. I really don't want to do a halfway job."

Kat was tugging on his hand, wanting him to help her finish drawing a pony. He glanced down at his daughter and then back to the woman standing a short distance away. She was already moving around the kitchen, picking up trash and tossing it, putting dishes next to the sink. Long curls were held in a ponytail and she wore flip-flops with her jeans.

The shoes made a flap-flap sound on the tile

floors that distracted him for a second, until she cleared her throat.

"Upstairs, Wyatt?"

He glanced up, meeting brown eyes and a hint of a strawberry-glossed smile. Molly's hand slid into his and he squeezed lightly, holding her close, grounded by her presence and shifted back to reality by her shoulder against his leg.

Eighteen months of holding it together, just trying to be a dad and trying to make sense of life, and now this. This, meaning Rachel Waters and the sudden realization that he was still a man. He blinked a few times, surprised that he'd noticed anything other than the broom she held in her hand. When was the last time he'd noticed a woman's lips? Or her hair?

He'd seen her at church every Sunday, though. It wasn't the first time he'd noticed her, her smile, her laugh. It wasn't the first time she'd taken him by surprise.

"Yeah, sure, go ahead. The bedrooms are fine, though. The girls clean their own. Kind of." He grinned down at his daughters because that cleaning part was an exaggeration. "Anyway, there are a couple of bathrooms up there."

"Good, I'll clean those, too." She grabbed a broom and swept at his feet. "Scoot, now."

Scoot. Molly was already pulling him toward the

hall. He glanced back at Rachel. She had turned on the CD player hidden under the upper cabinets and in moments Sara Evans was singing about a runaway teen leaving the suds in the bucket and the clothes hanging on the line.

As his daughters led him down the hall to the office, he could hear the chorus of the song and Rachel singing along. Her voice got a little louder on the line about wondering what the preacher would preach about on Sunday. He shot a look back in the direction of the kitchen, but the wall blocked her from sight.

Kat was dragging him into the office, jabbering about ponies and wondering when she would get one of her own. She was two. He considered reminding her of that fact, but she'd been reminded more than once.

For the next couple of hours the girls colored pictures and he went over farm accounts and receipts for taxes that had to be filed. The vacuum cleaner rumbled overhead. Rachel was still singing. She was always singing. Even when he picked the girls up in the nursery at church he could hear her singing to them.

He should be glad about that, that someone sang to them, someone soft and feminine. And she laughed, all the time. At least with the kids she laughed. He tried to remember the last time he'd really laughed. He watched his daughters trade crayons and he remembered. Kat had done something that made him laugh. They laughed more than they had six months ago. Far more than they had a year ago.

He shook his head and glanced back at numbers blurring on the ledger he'd been staring at for the last hour. Ryder had just about let the ranch run into the ground. Not financially, just upkeep, the things that required sitting still.

His cell phone rang and he reached for it, distracted. Wendy's mom's voice said a soft hello. Mother-in-law? Did he still call her that? She was still grandmother to his girls. A week didn't pass that she didn't call to check on them. More than once a month she and William, her second husband, drove up from Oklahoma City to visit.

He didn't want to sound paranoid, but he thought it was more like spying. It was Violet's way of making sure he was surviving and that her granddaughters were being taken care of. He didn't really blame her. There had been a few months when he hadn't been sure if he was going to make it.

"Violet, how are you?"

"I'm fine, of course. The question is, how are you?" The southern accent should have been sweet and maternal. Instead it held about a dozen questions pertaining to his sanity.

Which was just fine.

"Good, Violet. The girls are coloring pictures and we're getting ready to eat lunch." He glanced at his watch and winced. It was past time for lunch.

"Isn't it a little late for lunch?" She never missed a thing. He smiled.

"A little, but we ate a late breakfast." That probably didn't sound better, but he wasn't going to lie to her.

"Right. Well, I thought I'd come up this week, just to…"

"Check up on us?"

"Of course not. Wyatt, you know we love you and the girls. I miss…"

Broken sentences. He held back the sigh. In the last eighteen months they'd talked in broken sentences, half-finished thoughts and unspoken accusations.

"I miss her, too." He finished the sentence for her.

"So, about this week?"

It wasn't a good week for a visit. He leaned back in his chair and stared out the window at the overgrown lawn. He needed to hire a lawn service. "Sure, Violet, I'll be here."

The vacuum cleaner stopped.

"What's that noise?" Violet asked.

"Ryder hired a housekeeper."

"Oh. Well, that's good."

"I guess it is."

"And a cook?"

Of course it came back to cooking. He smiled a little. "I don't need a cook."

She didn't respond for a minute. "Okay, Wyatt. Well, I'll call and let you know what day I'll be up."

No, she wouldn't. He slipped the phone back in his pocket knowing full well she'd launch a sneak attack when he least expected it.

He leaned to kiss Molly on the top of her head. "You girls stay here for a second. I'm going to talk to Miss Rachel and then we'll blow up our balloons. Later we'll go to town."

To the store for groceries and a cookbook for dummies. Maybe he could learn to cook before Violet showed up.

Molly shot him a narrow-eyed look. Kat ignored him. The girls were like night and day. Molly was her mother all over, but she looked like him. Kat looked like Wendy. They both had dark hair, but Kat's was a little lighter and she had Wendy's light brown eyes. It was getting easier to stare into eyes that reminded him of his wife.

He hurried up the stairs and met Rachel in the hallway. She picked up her bucket of cleaning supplies and then smiled at him. Perspiration glistened on her brow and her hair was a little damp. But the upstairs smelled clean for the first time in a long time.

The windows gleamed at either end of the hall and there were no cobwebs clinging to the ceiling. Maybe a housekeeper wasn't such a bad idea. It might be a great idea. But he didn't know if Rachel Waters was the one he wanted. She wore faded jeans and had the tiniest butterfly at the small of her back. Shouldn't a housekeeper wear something more…housekeeperish?

He pictured Alice from *The Brady Bunch*. Or the robot maid from *The Jetsons*. Yeah, that's what a housekeeper should look like. A housekeeper should make PB and J sandwiches and smell like joint cream, not wildflowers.

"Is there anything else I need to do?" She stood in the center of the hallway, the bucket in her hand, and he'd lost it for a minute.

"No, nothing else." He glanced around. "It looks great, though."

"I'm glad you approve. Listen, I know this isn't what you wanted, but if you ever need me to come over again, just call. I can even watch the girls if you need time away."

Time away from his girls. He needed that less than anything. He needed them with him, all the time. He didn't ever want them to be alone and afraid again. She didn't know that, though. There were details that no one knew but Wyatt, Andie and a few others. He'd left Florida to escape those memories. Florida, where he and Wendy had been in youth ministry after college.

"Thanks, I appreciate that. I don't usually leave them, other than in the church nursery. But I do have to head out in a few minutes and I wanted to make sure Ryder paid you enough."

"He did." She brushed strands of damp hair back from her face. "Are you sure you don't want me to stay with the girls?"

"No, I'll take them. I'm just going to the store."

Because he had separation anxiety and so did they. It was about the least manly statement he could think of to make, so he didn't. He glanced out the window, which gleamed and the finger-prints the girls had put on the glass were gone.

She smiled. "Okay, but the offer stands."

"Thanks."

Rachel headed down the stairs with the bucket. He followed. Her shirt stayed carefully in place. He kind of hoped…and then again, he didn't. He shook his head and worked hard to pull it together.

She stopped at the bottom of the stairs. The girls ran out of the office, pigtails and sunshine. His sunshine. He hugged them both close. But they broke out of his arms and ran to Rachel. She didn't hesitate, just pulled them close and hugged them as she kissed the tops of their heads.

His phone rang again, not a moment too soon because he needed the distraction from the scene in front of him. Rachel walked away with his girls. He watched them as he raised the phone to his ear.

"Wyatt, how did you like your surprise?" Ryder laughed from five hundred miles away.

"Thanks."

"Is she done cleaning?"

"Yeah, the house looks great. I'm going to think of a nice surprise for you when you get back."

"You should be more appreciative. You have a clean house and a pretty woman to clean it."

"I wouldn't talk like that in front of my wife if I was you."

"She knows I only have eyes for her. But you, on the other hand…"

"Ever heard of the word *subtle,* little brother?"

Ryder laughed, louder, longer. Wyatt held the phone away from his ear.

"I guess subtle has never been my thing," Ryder admitted.

"Listen, I have to go shopping. Remind me that I owe you for this. And the payback won't be pleasant."

Rachel walked toward him, the laughter gone from her dark eyes and he didn't even know why. He couldn't let that be his problem. He had enough girl problems. One was two and the other was almost four. They were more than enough to keep him busy and keep him guessing.

"I'm going now." She stared straight at him, her gaze unwavering. She had a few freckles on sun-tanned cheeks.

"Okay, well, thank you." He didn't have time for this. "Look, I appreciate what you did. The place looks great. I just…"

"Don't need a housekeeper?"

He shrugged off the sarcasm in her tone. They both knew that he needed a housekeeper. What he didn't need was that little smile of hers making him feel as if he needed a housekeeper and an intervention.

"Yeah, I don't need a housekeeper." It hadn't been what he'd planned to say, but it worked.

What he really didn't need was someone who smelled like spring and who reminded him of everything he'd lost.

Chapter Two

Rachel drove away from the Johnson ranch and she was pretty glad to see it in her rearview mirror. She wanted to be a good distance away before the girls released the balloons with messages to their mother. It wouldn't have done anyone any good to have Rachel crying by their side.

She really should have known that she wouldn't be able to do this, spend more time with them, and stay detached. After years of considering herself a real pro at detachment, two little girls and a cowboy were going to be her downfall. The signs had been pretty obvious. The girls had been in the nursery and her preschool Sunday school class for six months and it had been way easy to fall in love with them.

Of course Wyatt wasn't included in those emotions. She felt sorry for him, nothing else. After hearing his conversation with Ryder, she knew he felt about the same for her.

It shouldn't matter to her what he thought. At twenty-nine, when she finally knew who she was and what she wanted out of life, Wyatt Johnson's opinion shouldn't matter. But old feelings of inadequacy didn't care what she thought of herself now. Those old emotions had a way of pushing to the surface when she least needed them.

So what? She would never be homecoming queen and guys like Wyatt Johnson always laughed behind her back.

It didn't matter anymore. She wasn't the fat girl in school or the rebel in the back of a police car trying to prove to people that she wasn't the good little preacher's kid.

She knew who she was, and who God wanted her to be. She worked in children's ministry, helped when her mother's lupus flared, and she loved her life in Dawson.

All of those pretty sermons to herself didn't take away a sudden desire for a big, fat chocolate bar. Or brownies with ice cream. She reached for her purse and dug her hand through the side pocket for a pack of gum. As she drove she managed to get a stick of peppermint gum out of the package.

She shoved the gum in her mouth and chewed,

trying to pretend it helped the way chocolate helped. It didn't.

Forget Wyatt, she had other things to do. She was supposed to work for Etta Forrester that afternoon. Etta designed and sewed a line of tie-dye clothing that she sold to specialty boutiques around the country. Etta made sundresses, skirts, pants, tops and even purses. Rachel worked for her a couple of days a week, more if Etta needed. With Etta's granddaughter, Andie, married to Ryder Johnson and Andie's twin, Alyson, married to Jason Bradshaw, Etta had more need for help these days.

She drove down the road and pulled into Etta's driveway. The bright yellow Victorian with the lavender wicker furniture on the wide porch managed to lift Rachel's spirits. Etta stood on the porch with a watering can in her hand and a floppy hat covering her lavender-gray hair. She waved as she poured water on the flowers. Last week she'd made a trip to Grove and she'd come home with a truck load of plants for the baskets and flower gardens.

Rachel parked under the shade of an oak tree and stepped out of her car. As she walked up the wide steps of the porch, Etta put down the watering can and pulled off her gardening gloves. Her nails were long, painted purple and never chipped. It was a mystery how Etta could take care of this farm, make her clothing and always be perfectly manicured.

The one time Rachel asked how she did it, Etta laughed and said, "Oh, honey, life teaches those little skills."

Rachel doubted it. She always felt about as together as a pair of old shoes falling apart at the seams. She couldn't paint her nails without smudging at least one. And her hair. The only good thing that had ever happened to her hair was a ponytail holder.

"Good to see you, honey." Etta slipped an arm around Rachel's shoulders. "I thought we'd have tea out here before we get started on those T-shirts."

"Tea sounds wonderful."

"You look about wrung out. Did you clean Wyatt's house today?"

Rachel nodded and picked dead blooms off the petunias.

Etta lifted her sunglasses and stared hard. "Well, tell me how it went."

"The place was definitely a mess." She shrugged and kept plucking blooms, tossing them over the rail into the yard. "And so is Wyatt."

"Oh, he isn't such a mess. He just needs a little time." Etta lifted the little watch she wore on a chain around her neck. "Goodness, speaking of time. I'm going to keep watering. Do you want to bring the tea out?"

"I can do that."

Etta had lowered the sunglasses. The big rhinestone encrusted frames covered half her face. "And try not to look so down in the mouth, honey. You're going to depress me and you know I don't depress easily."

Rachel smiled. "Is that better?"

"Not much." Etta laughed and went back to watering.

"I'll be back in a few."

"I'll be here."

The dog that had been sleeping under a tree started barking as Rachel fixed the tea tray. She picked up the wooden tray and headed down the hallway to the front door. The door was open and a breeze lifted the curtains in the parlor. Voices carried on that breeze.

"So you think you're going to learn to cook something more than canned spaghetti and hamburgers?" Etta laughed and said something else that Rachel didn't hear.

She stopped at the screen door and looked out. Etta was standing on the sidewalk and Wyatt stood next to her. Etta's skirt flapped in the breeze. Wyatt had taken off his hat and held it behind his back.

They were both facing the opposite direction and didn't see Rachel.

"It can't be that hard to learn, Etta. I've got to show Violet that I'm capable."

"Of course you're capable." Etta turned and waved when she saw Rachel. "There's Rachel with my tea. Well, have a seat and while you have tea, I'll look for a cookbook."

"I appreciate it, Etta, but I don't have time for tea. The girls are waiting in the truck. We're going grocery shopping."

Etta argued, of course she did. "Well, get the girls out."

Wyatt laughed, white teeth flashing in a kind of hot smile. He shook his head. "I'm not getting them out of the truck. If I do, I'll never round them up and get them back in the truck. I just thought rather than taking my chance with any old cookbook I found in the store, I'd see if you had one that spelled it all out."

Etta held the rail and walked up the steps, Wyatt following. "I'll see what I have. Something with casseroles would be best."

"If I can throw the whole meal in one pan, I guess that would be the best thing."

"You ought to know how to cook, Wyatt. It isn't like you're a kid."

"I never thought much about it, Etta." His neck turned a little red. "I guess I always thought…"

Etta's eyes misted and she patted his arm. "I'll be right back. I'll pick you out a couple and you'll be cooking us dinner in no time."

After Etta walked away, Rachel didn't know what to say. She hadn't been at a loss for words in years. Probably about twenty-eight of them. Her mom liked to tell people that she was talking in complete sentences when she was two and that she'd been talking ever since.

But at that moment she was pretty near speechless and so was Wyatt Johnson.

"My mother-in-law is coming to visit." He had placed the cowboy hat back on his head. He leaned against the rail of the porch, tall and confident. His boots were scuffed and his jeans were faded and worn in spots.

How many people would guess that the Johnson brothers had part ownership of a bank in Tulsa and subdivisions named after their family? She only knew those things because Andie, Wyatt's sister-in-law and Etta's granddaughter, had told her. Andie had married Ryder Johnson before Christmas and their twin babies were due in a month or so.

"I see." She nearly offered to help, and then she

didn't. She'd already told him she'd clean or watch the girls. He'd rejected both offers.

"She's worried that I'm not coping." His smile lifted one corner of his mouth and he shrugged. "I guess it won't hurt me or the girls to have a home-cooked meal once in a while."

"I imagine it won't." Rachel poured her tea. "Do you want a cup?"

"No, thanks. I like my tea on ice and out of a glass that holds more than a swallow."

She smiled and listened for Etta's footsteps. Etta would give him a long lecture if she heard him demean her afternoon tea ritual.

It was a few minutes before Etta appeared, her arms holding more than a few cookbooks. "Here's a few to get you started."

"That's a half dozen, Etta, not a few."

"Well, you can find what you really like this way."

He took the books from her arms. "Thanks, Etta. Rachel, see you at church."

He nodded to each of them and walked down the steps.

The truck was pulling down the driveway when Etta laughed a little and whistled. "That's tension you could cut with a knife."

"What?" Rachel nearly poured Etta's tea on the table.

"The two of you, circling like a couple of barn cats. I'm no expert, but I think it's called chemistry."

"I think it's called, Wyatt knows that everyone, including his brother, is trying to push me off on him."

"And would that be such a bad thing?" Etta sat down on the lavender wicker settee.

"I'm not sure, but I think he believes it probably would be."

"What about you?"

Rachel sipped her tea and ignored the question. Etta smiled and her brows shot up, but Rachel didn't bite. No way, no how was she chasing after Wyatt Johnson or any other man, for that matter. She'd done her chasing, she'd had her share of fix-ups, and she'd learned that it worked better to let things happen the way they were supposed to happen.

Or not. But she had decided a long time ago that being alone was better than pushing her way into the life of the wrong person.

It had been two days since Rachel cleaned and his house still looked pretty decent. Wyatt stood in the kitchen with its dark cabinets, black granite countertops and stainless steel appliances. A chef's kitchen for a guy who had to borrow cookbooks because he couldn't make mac and cheese. That was pretty bad.

He hadn't planned it, but Rachel was front and center in his mind again. She was a strange one. First glance and he would have thought she had all the confidence in the world. But the other day on Etta's porch, there had been something soft and kind of lost in her expression, in those dark eyes of hers.

Not that it was any of his concern.

He dropped bread into the toaster and started the coffeemaker. Excited voices and little feet pattering overhead meant the girls were up. His day was about to start.

At least he'd had fifteen minutes to himself. That didn't happen often these days. It hadn't happened much in the last eighteen months. Since Wendy left him.

He stopped in front of the kitchen window and looked out. For a minute he closed his eyes and remembered that he used to pray. He used to believe that with Wendy he could build a life far from this ranch and the chaos of his childhood. He opened his eyes and shook his head. Prayer these days was abbreviated. It went something like: *God, get me through another day.*

That would have to do for now. It was all he had in him, other than anger and guilt.

Eighteen months of trying to figure out what he could have done differently. He was still trying to come to terms with the reality that he couldn't have done anything more than he'd done. Wendy had made a choice.

The choice to leave him and their daughters. She wrote a note, opened a bottle of sleeping pills and she'd left them for good.

Eighteen months of wondering what he could have done to stop her from going away.

He breathed in deep and it didn't hurt as much as yesterday, even less than a month ago. He was making it. He had to make it—for the girls. He had to smile and make each day better for them. And he calculated that he had about two minutes before they hit the kitchen, ready for breakfast. Two minutes to pull it together and make this day better.

On cue, they rushed in, still in their pajamas. Man, they made it easy to smile. He leaned to hug them and pulled them up to hold them both. He brushed his whiskered cheek against Kat and she giggled.

"What are we going to do today, girlies?"

"Get a pony!" Kat shouted and then she giggled some more.

"Nope, not a pony." He kissed her cheek.

"Let Miss Rachel clean again." Molly's tone was serious but her smile was real, her eyes shining. She knew how to work him.

He sat both girls on the granite-topped island that sat in the center of the kitchen. "Miss Rachel? Why do you want her to clean?"

He liked the idea of a clean house, but he was determined to find a nice grandmotherly type. He wanted control top socks and cookies baking in the oven. It sounded a lot less complicated than Miss Rachel I've-Got-Secrets Waters.

Kat sighed, as if he couldn't possibly be her dad or he would understand why they picked Rachel. She leaned close. "She hugs me."

"She draws pictures and sings." Molly crossed her arms and her little chin came up. "She has sheep."

"I'm sure she does. But she's really busy with church and helping Miss Etta."

"She doesn't mind cleaning." Molly was growing up and her tone said that she had a handle on this situation.

"Look, girls, she just cleaned for us that one time. Uncle Ryder hired her." He reached into the cabinet under the island and pulled out a cereal box. Add that to his list for the day. He needed to go to the store again. Even though he'd had a list, he'd forgotten a lot. "How about cereal?"

"And a pony?" Kat grinned and her eyes were huge.

A pony. Would it work to buy himself a break from this?

"Maybe a pony." He was so weak. "But first we have to eat breakfast and then we need to go outside and feed the horses and cows we already have."

He lifted them down from the counter and sat them each on a stool at the island.

"You girls are getting big."

Molly. He shook his head because she wasn't just big, she acted like an old soul, as if she'd had to learn too much too soon. And she had.

Most of it he doubted she remembered. If she did, the memories were vague. But she remembered being afraid. He knew she remembered that.

He took bowls out of the cabinet and set one in front of each girl and one for himself. He opened the cereal cabinet door again and looked at the half-dozen boxes. "Chocolate stuff, fruity stuff or kind-of-healthy stuff?"

The girls giggled a little.

"That does it, you get kind-of-healthy today. I think you've had way too much sugar because you're both so sweet." He grabbed the box and then reached for the girls and held them, kissing their cheeks. "Yep, sweet enough."

Normal moments, the kind a dad should share with his daughters. Eighteen long months of going through the motions, but they were all coming back to life. They were building something new here, in this house. They would have good memories. He hadn't expected to have something good for his family here, in Dawson. His own dad hadn't provided that for him and Ryder.

But he wasn't his dad. He guessed he learned something from his dad's mistakes. Like how to be faithful. And how to be there.

His phone rang and he answered it as he poured cereal into three bowls. Two partially filled and his to the top. He talked as he poured milk and dug in a drawer for spoons. When he hung up both girls were looking at him.

"I have to go pick up something for Uncle Ryder." He ate his cereal standing across the counter from the girls.

"A pony?" Kat giggled as she spooned cereal into her mouth. Milk dribbled down her chin and her brown eyes twinkled.

"No, a bull."

"We can go?" Molly didn't touch her cereal and he knew, man, he knew how scared she was.

He was just starting to get over it, *he* hadn't been a two-year-old kid alone with a mommy who wouldn't wake up.

That kind of fear and pain changed a person. Molly was watching him, waiting for him to be the grown-up, the one who smiled and showed her that it was okay to be happy.

"Of course you can go." He took a bite of cereal and she followed his example. She even smiled. He let out a sigh that she didn't hear.

Fifteen minutes later he walked out the back door with them on his heels. Today they'd slipped back into the old pattern of leaving dishes on the counter and dirty clothes on the floor in the bedroom. He didn't have time to worry about it right now. He'd barely had time to pull on his boots and find his hat.

Horses saw him and whinnied. The six mares in the field closest to the house headed toward their feed trough. He whistled and in the other field about a dozen horses lifted their heads and headed toward the barn, ready for grain.

A quick glance over his shoulder confirmed that Kat and Molly were close behind him. They weren't right on his heels now, but they were following, grabbing up dandelions and chasing after the dog.

He turned away from the girls and headed for

the fence. He watched for a chestnut mare. She walked a short distance behind the others. Her limp was slight today. She'd gotten tangled in old barbed wire out in the field. Sometimes a good rain washed up a lot of junk from the past.

This mare had stepped into that junk one day last week after a gully washer of a rain. He'd found her with gashes in her fetlock and blood still oozing from the wound. She headed for the fence and him, the extra attention over the last week had turned her into a pet.

A car driving down the road honked. He turned to wave. The red convertible slowed and pulled into his drive. The girls hurried to his side, jabbering about Rachel's car. He had worked hard at building a safe life for his girls.

What was it about Rachel that shook it all up? He glanced down at his girls and they didn't look too scared.

He tossed the thought aside. Rachel was about the safest person in the world. She was a Sunday school teacher and the preacher's daughter.

So what part of her life had been crazy enough for butterfly tattoos?

Rachel had meant to drive on past the Johnson ranch, but the girls waving dandelions had done it for her. She had seen them from a distance, first noticing the horses running for the fence and then spotting Wyatt and his girls. She had slowed to watch and then she'd turned.

As she pulled up to the barn she told herself this was about the craziest thing she'd done since... She had to think about it and one thing came to mind. The tattoo.

She'd thought about having it removed, but she kept it to remind herself to make decisions based on the future and not the moment. So what in the world was she doing here, at Wyatt Johnson's? He probably wanted her around as much as she wanted to be there.

This was definitely a spontaneous decision and not one that was planned out. Stupid. Stupid. Stupid.

The girls dropped the dandelions and raced across the lawn, the dog at their heels. As she pushed her door open, Molly and Kat were there, little faces scrubbed clean and smiles bright. No matter what, he'd done a great job with the girls, even if he did seem to be color-blind. That had to be the reason the girls never seemed to have an outfit that matched.

This time they were in their pajamas.

"What are you girls up to?"

"We're going with Daddy." Molly held tight to her hand.

Wyatt had disappeared. Into the barn, she

decided. She could hear him talking and heard a door shut with a thud. He walked back out, his hat pulled down to block the sun from his face. He had a bag of grain tossed over his shoulder, his biceps bulging.

She let the girls tug her hands to follow him. He stopped at a gate and unlatched it with his free hand. Cattle were at a trough, waiting. From outside the fence she watched him yank the string on the top of the bag and pour it down the length of the trough. He walked back with the empty bag. After closing the gate he tossed the bag into a nearby barrel.

And then he was staring at her. The hat shaded his face, but it definitely didn't hide the questions in his dark eyes. And she didn't have answers. What could she tell him, that her car suddenly had a mind of its own? But she'd have to think of something because the girls were pulling her in his direction.

"What are you up to today?" He pulled off leather gloves and shoved them in the back pocket of his jeans.

She didn't have an answer. The girls were holding her hands and she was staring into the dark eyes of a man who had been hurt to the deepest level. And survived. Those eyes were staring her down, waiting for an answer.

She was on his territory. She'd never felt it more than at that moment, that territorial edge of his. He protected the ones he loved.

"I saw the girls and I realized you might not know about our church picnic Wednesday evening. Instead of our normal service, we're roasting hot dogs and marshmallows."

It wasn't a lie, she had forgotten to remind him. He seemed to need reminding from time to time. He had a degree in ministry and yet church seemed to be something he forced himself to do. She got that. She had done her share of avoiding church, too.

He'd actually been in youth ministry until eighteen months ago.

"Sounds like fun." He glanced at his watch.

"I should go. Listen, if you need anything, any more help around here…"

"Right, I'll let you know."

She should have known better than to think he'd want to talk. A momentary glitch in her good sense had made her believe that he might want a friend. But then, he probably had friends. He'd grown up here.

"See you two Wednesday." Time to walk away.

Kat grabbed her hand. "Come and see my frog."

"Kat, you don't have a frog." Wyatt reached for

her but Kat pulled Rachel the other direction and two-year-olds were pretty strong when they had their mind set on something.

"I have a frog." She didn't let go and Rachel didn't have the heart to tell her no. She went willingly in the direction of an old log.

"Is that where your frog lives?"

"There are millions of frogs." Kat dropped to her knees and pushed the chunk of wood. Sure enough, little frogs hopped out. Actually, they were baby toads. She didn't correct the toddler.

"Wow, Kat, there are a bunch of them." Rachel kneeled next to the child. "Do you have names for them?"

Kat nodded. "But I don't 'member."

"I think they're beautiful. I bet they like living under this log."

Kat nodded, her eyes were big and curls hung in her eyes. Rachel pushed the hair back from the child's face and Kat smiled. A shadow loomed over them. Kat glanced up and Rachel turned to look up at Wyatt. He was smiling down at his daughter. The smile didn't include Rachel.

He had a toe-curling smile, though, and she wanted her toes to curl. Which was really just plain wrong.

"Kat, we have to go, honey." He got hold of

Molly's hand. "I have to finish feeding and you two need to be getting ready to jump in the truck."

"We're getting a pony." Kat patted Rachel's cheek with a dirty hand that had just released a toad back to its home under the log.

"Are you?" She looked up and Wyatt shook his head.

"We're picking up a bull."

"I see." Rachel stood and dusted off her jeans. "I could stay here with them, Wyatt."

She had offered the other day and he'd said no, so why in the world was she offering again? Oh, right, because she loved, loved, loved rejection. And to make it better, she loved that look on his face when his eyes narrowed and he looked at her as if she had really fallen off the proverbial turnip truck.

He took in a breath and she wondered why it was so hard for him to leave them. "No, they can go with me."

"But we could stay, and Miss Rachel could help us draw pictures." Molly bit down on rosy lips and big tears welled up in her eyes. "I always get carsick."

"I'm sorry, I shouldn't have said anything."

"That's a thought." Wyatt picked up his little girl. "Molly, you're going with me."

She nodded and rested her head on his shoulder.

"I'll see you later." Rachel brushed a hand down Molly's little back.

Yes, driving up here had been the wrong thing to do. She leaned to kiss Kat's cheek and then she walked away. She had a life. She had things to do today. She definitely didn't need to get tied up in the heartache that was Wyatt Johnson's life.

She made it to her car without looking back.

Wyatt put Molly down and he held tight to Kat's hand because he had a feeling that if he let go, she was going to run after Rachel. Molly was looking up at him, as if she was wondering why in the world he wasn't the one running after her new favorite person.

He needed this as much has he needed to hit his thumb with a hammer. If God would give him a break, he'd get the hammer and hit his thumb twice.

He wasn't going to run after a woman, not one who made more trouble in his life. And that's what she was doing. She was causing him a lot of trouble. She was upsetting the organized chaos of his life with her sunny personality and cute little songs.

She was getting in her car and Kat was next to him, begging him to stop her. He stared at the preacher's daughter in jean shorts and a T-shirt.

Not for himself, for Kat. Man, he didn't need this. He let go of his daughter's hand and went after Rachel. Yelling when she started her car. Waving for her to stop when she put it in reverse.

The radio was blasting from the convertible. She loved music. He shook his head because today she was listening to Taylor Swift and a song about teen romance gone wrong. He really didn't need this.

She had stopped and she turned the radio down and waited for him to get to her. This was proof that he'd do anything for his girls. He'd even put up with Miss Merry Sunshine for a couple of hours if it made Molly and Kat smile.

When he reached the car she turned and lifted her sunglasses, pushing them on top of her head. He realized that her eyes were darker than he'd thought, and bigger. They were soft and asked questions.

"The girls really want you to go with us. I thought it might help. They'll be bored if this takes too long."

She just stared at him.

"I'll pay you," he offered with a shrug that he hoped was casual and not as pathetic as he imagined.

She laughed and the sound went through him. "Pay me?"

"For watching them."

She was going to make him beg. He shoved his hat down a little tighter on his head and then loosened it.

"You don't have to pay me. It would be kind of fun to see that bull. Is it one they'll use for bull riding?"

"Yeah, probably."

"Fun. Where should I park?"

He pointed to the carport near the barn. "That'll keep it a little cooler. I have to finish feeding and the girls have to get dressed."

"Can I help?"

Hadn't she helped enough?

"No, I can do it." He walked away because it was a lot easier than staying there to answer more of her questions. He knew it probably seemed rude, but she didn't have a clue.

She didn't know that he was rebuilding his family and that it took every bit of energy he had. Everything he had went to his girls, into making them smile and making their lives stable.

As he walked into the barn he glanced back. She leaned to talk to Kat. Curls fell forward, framing her face, but a hand came up to push her hair back. She smiled and leaned to kiss his daughter on the cheek. And then the three of them, Rachel, Kat and Molly, headed into the house.

He walked into the shadowy interior of the barn and flipped on a light. He breathed in the familiar scents. Cows, horses, hay and leather. He could deal with this. He couldn't deal with Mary Poppins.

Chapter Three

If it hadn't been for Kat and Molly she wouldn't have climbed into this truck and taken a ride with Wyatt. But the girls, with their sweet smiles and tight hugs, they were what mattered. Little girls should never hurt. They shouldn't hide their pain in cheesecake or think their self-worth depended on the brand and size of their jeans.

Oh, wait, that had been her, her childhood, her pain.

"You aren't carsick, are you?" Wyatt's voice was soft, a little teasing. Yummier than cheesecake. And she hadn't had cheesecake in forever.

She glanced his way and smiled. "I don't get carsick."

"Good to know. The girls do. Not on roads like this, fortunately."

"We keep a trash can back here." Molly informed

her with the voice of young authority. Rachel heard the tap, tap of a tiny foot on plastic.

She looked over her shoulder at the two little girls on the bench seat behind her. Kat's eyes were a little droopy and she nodded, her head sagging and then bouncing up. Molly looked as if she had a lot more to say but she was holding back.

Poor baby girls. Wyatt loved them, but there was an empty space in their lives that a mom should have filled. And they wouldn't even have memories of her as they grew older. They would have pictures and stories their dad told.

If he told stories. She chanced a quick glance in his direction and thought he probably didn't tell stories about the wife he'd lost. He probably had a boat load of memories he wished he could lose.

"Here we are." He flipped on the turn signal and smiled at her as he pulled into a gated driveway. "Can you pull through and I'll open the gate?"

"I can open the gate." She reached for the door handle and opened it, ignoring his protests. It was a lot easier to be outside away from him. A soft breeze blew in warm spring air and she could hear cattle at a nearby dairy farm.

She loved Oklahoma. Growing up she'd lived just about everywhere, but mostly in bigger towns and cities. She'd never felt like she belonged. Maybe because she had always been the pastor's kid, poor in wealthy subdivisions, trying to fit in. Or maybe because deep down she'd always wanted to be a country girl.

She had wanted to jump out of trucks and open gates. She had studied about sheep, wool and gardening. Pitiful as it sounded, she'd watched so many episodes of *The Waltons,* she could quote lines. She couldn't think about it now without smiling.

The truck eased through the gate and stopped. She pushed the gate closed and latched the chain. When she climbed back into the truck, Wyatt wasn't smiling.

"I said I'd get it." He shifted into gear and the truck eased forward again.

"I don't mind."

"No, you don't."

Oh, no, he hadn't! She shot him a look. "I'm not five. I don't mind opening gates. I really don't have to *mind* you."

His brows went up. He reached for the hat he'd set on the seat next to him and pushed it back on his head. The chicken wasn't going to comment. She glanced back at the girls and smiled. Kat was sleeping. Molly stared out the window, her eyelids drooping.

Wyatt parked next to the barn, still silent. But when she glanced his way, she saw the smile. It barely lifted the corners of his mouth, but it was there.

"This shouldn't take long." He opened his door and paused. "I think you and the girls can get out and look around."

"Thanks, we'll do that. If you think I can handle it. After all, I'm five."

"You're not five. You're just…" He shook his head and got out of the truck. He didn't say anything else. He opened the back door of the truck and motioned for the girls to get out. He set each of them on the ground and then glanced back in at her. "Getting out?"

"Yeah, I'm getting out."

She'd been crazy to stop at his house. She was still trying to figure it out. He smiled at something Kat said. Oh, that's right, now she remembered. It was that smile. She wanted him to smile like that at her.

"Wyatt, good to see you."

She turned to face the man who'd spoken. He stood outside the barn and everything about him said "rancher." From his dusty boots to his threadbare jeans, he was a cowboy. His skin was worn and suntanned, making deeper lines around his mouth and crinkles at his eyes. His hair was sunstreaked brown. He winked at her.

"Jackson, I'm surprised to see you here. I thought

your brother was meeting me." Wyatt stepped toward the other man, hand extended.

"Yeah, he's at the bank. You know, he's Mr. Workaholic."

"Got it. So what are you doing these days?"

"Oh, trying to stay away from trouble. But most of the time, trouble just seems to find me." He smiled at Rachel. "Hi there, Trouble."

Heat climbed her cheeks.

"Jackson Cooper, meet Rachel Waters. Her father is the pastor of the Dawson Community Church."

If Wyatt had used that introduction to put the other man in his place, Jackson Cooper didn't look at all embarrassed. "If our pastor's daughter looked like you, I might just get right with God."

Wyatt wasn't smiling. "Okay, let's look at the bull."

"You gonna ride him?" Jackson laughed.

"I doubt it."

"Chicken?" Jackson Cooper obviously didn't know about backing down. She thought it might be a family trait; not backing down. She had heard about the Coopers. There were about a dozen of them: biological and adopted.

"Nope, just smarter than I used to be. I haven't been on a bull in a half-dozen years and I don't plan on starting again."

"There's a lot more money in it these days," Jackson continued, his smile still in place.

"Plenty of money in raising them, too." Wyatt turned to his daughters. "You girls stay with Rachel and I'll be back in a few minutes."

The men left them and Rachel smiled down at the girls. "I think we should make clover chains."

One last glance over her shoulder. Wyatt picked that moment to stop and watch them, to watch his girls. Rachel turned away.

"Nice bull." Young, but definitely worth the money the Coopers were asking. Wyatt watched the young animal walk around the corral. He was part Brahma, long and rangy with short legs. He'd been used in local rodeos last year and was already on the roster for some bigger events.

"Want me to get a bull rope and chaps?" Jackson leaned over the corral, a piece of straw in his mouth.

"No, I think we know what he'll do. And we know where you live if he doesn't."

"He'll go out of the chute to the right for about four spins and then switch back and spin left. He's got a belly roll you won't believe."

"Your brother, Blake, told Ryder that he isn't mean." Wyatt continued to watch the bull. The animal pushed at an old tire and then stomped the dusty ground.

"He's never hurt anyone. But he's a bull, Wyatt. They're unpredictable, we both know that."

"Yeah, I know we do." They'd lost a friend years ago. They'd been teenagers riding in junior events when Jimmy got killed at a local event.

"That was a rough one, wasn't it?" Jackson's sister had dated Jimmy.

"Yeah, it was rough." He brushed away the memories. "Do I write you a check?"

"Sure. So, is she your nanny?" Jackson nodded in the direction of Rachel Waters. She was in the large yard and the girls were with her. They were picking clover and Rachel slipped a chain of flowers over Molly's head.

Wendy should have been there, doing those things with their daughters. He let out a sigh and refocused on the bull. It took a minute to get his thoughts back on track. Jackson didn't say anything.

"No, she isn't." Wyatt pulled the checkbook out of his back pocket. "I like the bull, Jackson. I don't like your price."

Jackson laughed. "Well, now, Wyatt, I don't know that I care if you like my price or not."

"He isn't worth it and you know it."

"So what do you think would make him worth

it?" Jackson's smile disappeared. Yeah, that was the way to wipe good-natured off a guy's face, through his bank account.

"I've been thinking of adding Cooper Quarter Horses to our breeding program. I'd like one of your fillies." His gaze swept the field and landed on a small herd of horses. One stuck out, but it wasn't quite what he'd planned to ask for. "And that pony."

"You want a pony. Shoot, Wyatt, I'll throw in the pony. We'll have to talk about the horse, though. This bull's daddy was Bucking Bull of the Year two years in a row. He isn't a feedlot special."

"Okay, let's talk." Wyatt let his gaze slide to where the girls were still playing with Rachel. Kat was sitting on the grass, a big old collie next to her. Molly and Rachel were spinning in circles.

They needed her. The thought settled so deep inside of him that it ached. His girls needed Rachel. Maybe more than they needed him. He couldn't make chains with clover or even manage a decent braid in their hair.

"Do you think she'd go out with me?" Jackson walked over to the gate and tugged it open. "I mean, if you're not interested."

"I'm not interested." Wyatt walked through the gate, sidestepping a little snake that slid past. "I'm not interested, but I think maybe you're not her type. Shoot, I'm probably not her type either."

"Yeah, well, I always had this idea that when I settle down it'd be with a woman like her, the kind that goes to church on Sundays and probably makes a mean roast." Jackson shot him a smile. "Yeah, a guy would live right with a wife like her."

"Right." He'd had enough of this talk. "Let's take a look at the pony first. How old?"

"Ten. He was my niece's. But Tash is getting older and Greg bought her a bigger horse."

"I don't want to take someone's pony."

"He's just eating grass and getting fat."

Wyatt stopped in front of the paint pony. It was a pretty thing, brown and white spotted with a black mane and tail. The pony lifted its head from the clover that it was munching on and gave him a look.

"He isn't mean?"

"Never seen him be mean."

Wyatt knew all about horse traders and lines like that. He wasn't about to take Jackson Cooper's word for it. He patted the fat pony and leaned against him, holding his mane to keep him close.

"Yeah, but I want a little more reassurance than that, Jackson. This is for my kids."

Jackson walked up and lifted a leg to settle it

over the pony's back. His normal smile had disappeared and he was all serious. "Wyatt, I might be a lot of things, but I can tell you this: I wouldn't get a kid hurt. This pony is the safest one you'll find. I broke him myself and I wouldn't be afraid to let my own kids on him. If I had a kid."

Wyatt nodded and he didn't take his eyes off the pony. Even with part of Jackson's weight on his back, the little pony hadn't moved, hadn't been distracted from the clover he was tugging at. He didn't even startle when shouts from the gate meant that he'd been spotted by the girls.

The girls were on the gate, standing midway up, waving. Rachel stood next to them, her smile as big as theirs. He wondered if she was still dreaming of having a pony someday? He'd known girls like her his whole life. Wannabe cowgirls. He used to like them. They were fun on a Friday night at a rodeo in Tulsa. They were easy to impress and soft to hold.

That had been a lifetime and another Wyatt Johnson ago. Before. His life fell into two slots. Before Wendy, and after. The first half had been full of hope and promise. The second was about getting it back.

He was just standing there, staring, when Jackson waved them into the field. They yelled and before Rachel could open the gate, they were running toward him. The little pony looked up, watching, dark ears pricked forward. Yeah, he'd do for a first pony.

Rachel caught up with the girls halfway across the field and spoke to them. He watched them settle and reach for her hands. One on each side of her.

Jackson whistled and shook his head, laughing a little. Wyatt shot him a sideways glance and shoved his hands in his pockets.

"Keep it to yourself, Jackson."

"I'm just saying…"

"Yeah, I know what you're saying." He wasn't blind.

And then the girls were there, Rachel standing quietly behind them. They were all hands, reaching for the pony, saying it was the prettiest pony ever. Jackson Cooper looked as if he had created the thing himself and set it in front of them with a ribbon.

"Be careful, girls." Rachel moved closer and her hand went out, reaching to brush through the pony's mane.

"What do you think, girls? Would this be a good pony?" Wyatt wanted to be the hero. He'd been fighting the pony conversation for a while. They were still little, still needed to be held and couldn't brush their teeth alone. He'd been on horses his entire life, but that was different. When it came to his girls, it was different.

Molly nodded. "This is a perfect pony named Prince."

"Actually, his name is..." Jackson grinned. "His name is Prince."

Rachel smiled at him. Wyatt lifted his hat and settled it back in place. "We'll take him. And a filly."

"Let's talk price." Jackson looped a bit of rope around the pony's neck. "Can you girls lead Prince back to the barn so we can load him in the trailer?"

Molly was nodding, her hands moving in anticipation, but Jackson handed the lead rope to Rachel. Wyatt started to tell them to be careful, but he clamped his mouth shut. He hadn't been real good at letting go lately. It wasn't easy, letting someone else take care of Molly and Kat. It wasn't easy watching them with someone who was not their mother.

But they needed this. They needed to let go of him once in a while.

His good intentions almost came undone when halfway to the gate Rachel stopped, picked up Molly and then Kat and placed them on the back of that pony. Kat was in front and Molly wrapped her arms around her sister. Rachel stood close to them.

"Might as well breathe and let it go, Wyatt." Jackson laughed and slapped him on the back. "Two things are going to happen. They're going to grow up, and that woman's probably going to get under your skin."

Wyatt didn't smile. He watched as Rachel led the pony with his girls on it through the gate and then he settled his attention back on Jackson Cooper and the filly he wanted.

And he repeated to himself that Rachel Waters wasn't going to get under his skin.

Chapter Four

Stupid moment number twelve. Or maybe twelve thousand? That's what Rachel thought of volunteering to ride along with Wyatt and the girls to get that bull. And it was even worse standing in the shade watching Wyatt unload the pony from the trailer. He had hauled the pony and his new filly home. He'd left the bull for Jackson Cooper to trailer for him.

The girls stood next to Rachel, waiting for their dad to give the all clear. They fidgeted in one spot because they knew better than to run at the pony.

Wyatt led the filly, a dark bay two-year-old, into the barn. The horse pranced alongside him, her black tail waving like a banner. The filly dipped her head a few times and whinnied to horses in the field who answered back with shrill whinnies to the new girl in town.

Wyatt walked out of the barn a few minutes later. The filly was still inside, her shrill whinny continued. Wyatt pulled off his hat and swiped his brow with his arm. The girls were tugging on Rachel's hands, but she didn't let go. Somehow she managed to stand her ground.

He had told them to wait. She was more than willing to do what he asked. She was content to stay in one spot and watch as he stepped back into the trailer to retrieve the pony.

The second he stepped out of the trailer with the pony the girls started to jabber. Kat was pulling on her hand. Rachel leaned and picked the child up. When she looked up, Wyatt watched, his smile gone, his expression unreadable. He turned away and led the pony to the small corral next to the barn.

He closed the gate and tied the lead rope to the pole fence. "Come on over."

She put down Kat and the girls ran toward him. He held up his hand and they slowed to a walk. Rachel followed because it was time to say goodbye. It had been a good day. The girls were wonderful. Wyatt was a wonderful dad who loved his daughters.

He probably thought Rachel could be a decent friend.

She'd had a lifetime of being the best friend,

the girl that guys called when they wanted a pal to hang out with. Funny that when she lost weight all of those best friends started looking at her in a different way.

Wyatt untied the lead rope. "If you want to hold her, I'll get the bridle and saddle."

"I can do that." So much for the quick escape. She took the rope and their fingers touched. She looked up, into dark eyes that held hers for a long moment. She looked away, back to the girls. Things that were easy.

Kat and Molly had climbed up on the bottom pole of the fence. They reached through and little fingers found the pony's mane.

"I'll be right back." Wyatt glanced from her to his daughters and then he walked away, disappearing through the side door of the barn.

And she should do the same. She should tell him she had things to do today. She needed to clean her room or weed the garden. There were plenty of things she could have been doing.

It might be a good idea for her to go home and spend time in prayer.

When he came back with the tiny saddle and bridle, she opened her mouth to explain that she should go. But he smiled and she stayed.

She stayed and held the little pony as Wyatt

lifted Kat and Molly onto his back. They rode double the first time, so that neither of them could say they got to ride first. Rachel stood by the gate watching as he led them around the corral. Kat was shaking the reins she held in her little hands, trying to make the pony run. Molly had her arms wrapped around her sister's waist and her smile was huge.

Wyatt lifted Molly off the saddle and put his hat on Kat's head. The black cowboy hat fell down over the child's eyes. She didn't mind. She had a pony.

Molly trudged across the arena and stopped next to Rachel. The little girl watched her sister ride the pony around the arena and as they got close, Molly started to bounce up and down.

"Might want to stand still, sweetie. We don't want to startle the pony," Rachel warned.

"Daddy said he didn't think a train going through would make him scared."

"He's a pretty special pony."

Molly looked up, her smile still splitting her little face. She nodded and continued to bounce as Wyatt headed their way with Kat in the saddle.

As he pulled one daughter down and lifted the other, Rachel stood close. "I should go now. Thank you for letting me go with you today."

Wyatt took the hat off Kat's head and placed it on Molly's. He turned to Rachel, his smile still in place. The hair at the crown of his head was flat from wearing the hat.

"Thanks for going. Are you sure you don't want a turn?" He teased with an Oklahoma drawl and a half smile.

"No, I think probably not. My feet would drag on the ground and the poor pony would need a chiropractor."

"I doubt that." He handed the reins to Molly. "Hold tight, kiddo."

"Have fun with the pony." Rachel leaned to kiss Kat's cheek and she waved to Molly the cowgirl. "See you at church Wednesday."

She turned to walk away, but Wyatt touched her arm, stopping her. She smiled because he looked as surprised as she did. His hand was still on her arm, warm and rough against her skin.

"All joking aside, I really do appreciate you going with us today. I know the girls loved having you along."

She shrugged and his hand slid off her arm. "I enjoyed it as much as they did."

And then she stood there, unmoving. The moment needed an escape route, the kind posted in hotel rooms. It should read: In case of emergency, exit here.

* * *

Wyatt remembered the Wednesday evening bonfire fifteen minutes before it started. He pulled into the parking lot of the church and the fire was already going, and people were gathered around in lawn chairs. He killed the engine on his truck and glanced in the backseat.

"Oh, man, we really should have done something with your hair." But the girls' hair had been the last thing on his mind as they rushed out the door.

He'd spent the day working the new bull, bringing it into the chute and bucking it out with a dummy on its back. He knew that it would buck, he just wanted to see for himself what they'd gotten themselves into. In the next week or two he'd take him over to Clint Cameron's and let some of the teens that hung out over there give him a try.

But the bull aside, he'd also had to put out a fire in the kitchen. A cooking experiment had gone very wrong. Good thing he'd remembered the Wednesday evening bonfire. He smiled at the girls. Both had dirty faces, pigtails that were coming undone and boots with their shorts. He was pretty sure this was a real fashion catastrophe.

At least they were at church. He got out and opened the back door for the girls. They clambered down from the truck, jumping off the running board and then heading off to join Rachel and the other kids.

She was the pied piper of girls, big and small. Teenagers followed her around, talking as she worked. Sometimes she gave them jobs to do. As he stared she glanced quickly in his direction.

"She's our bonus."

He turned and Etta smiled at him.

"What does that mean?" He shoved his keys in his pocket and walked across the big lawn with Etta. He thought to offer her his arm, but she would have laughed and told him she was able to walk on her own steam.

"I mean, we got a great pastor and pastor's wife and Rachel is the bonus. She does so much in the church. Our youth and children's ministries have doubled. That's why Pastor Waters is thinking of hiring a youth minister."

"I'm not interested."

"In Rachel you mean?" Etta smiled and headed in the other direction.

"You know what I mean." He called out after her. She turned and waved, ornery as ever. And he loved her. He thought back to the hard times in his life. She had been there, getting him through every one of them. She'd even flown down to Florida after Wendy died. She'd stayed a month, helping with babies, helping him to breathe.

"Wyatt."

This time it was Jason Bradshaw and his wife Alyson. The happy couple headed is his direction. There was too much romance going on in this town for his comfort.

"How are you two?"

"Good. I'm glad to see you here. We're going to have music after we eat. We can always use another guitar, if you have yours."

"I left it here last week." Wyatt scanned the yard for his girls.

He saw them in the playground. Molly had just gone down the slide. Kat had her arms around Rachel's neck and was being carried to the swing.

"Then I'll find you when we're ready to get started." Jason followed the direction of his gaze and smiled.

"Sounds good. I need to check on the girls."

"Right, check on the girls." Jason laughed and shot a pointed look in the direction of Rachel Waters.

Wyatt ignored the insinuation. He headed across the lawn toward the playground. Rachel sat on a bench, Molly in front of her. She had ponytail holders in her mouth and a brush in her hand. When he got close enough she looked up and smiled.

"Do you mind?"

He shook his head. "No."

But he did mind. For reasons he didn't get, he minded. It might have been about her, or about himself, maybe it was about Wendy, but he minded.

She scooted and he got that it was an offer. He could sit down and let people say what they wanted or he could walk away. And people would still talk. It wouldn't be malicious, the talk. No, it would be pure Dawson. Everyone would be hoping to fix him.

Option one seemed like the best bet. He sat down next to her. Kat hurried to him and climbed on his lap. Her hair had already been fixed. He hadn't noticed from across the lawn.

Molly sat quietly. She never sat that still for him. Rachel talked about their pony, talked about s'mores and ran the brush through his daughter's tangled brown hair. When it was smooth she pulled it back, brushed it smooth again and held it tight. She had placed the ponytail holders on her wrist and she took them off, wrapping them around the ponytail, holding it firm at the crown of Molly's head.

"There you go, sweetie." Rachel kissed her cheek.

"You make it look easy."

She smiled at the comment. "It takes practice. You'll get the hang of it."

He wasn't so sure.

After cooking hot dogs and marshmallows in the fire, Rachel sat with the kids, making a circle around Jason, Wyatt and some others. The men started with a few praise songs and then switched to contemporary Christian music. The teens clapped and sang along.

Molly and Kat climbed into her lap, both of them snuggling close. She held them tight and pretended it didn't hurt. But it did. The other children had gone off to their mommies.

Molly and Kat had turned to her while their daddy sang. She wrapped them in an extra blanket her own mother had brought and the two dozed in her lap. Firelight flickered. The songs were softer, sweeter. She closed her eyes and listened.

When she opened her eyes her gaze sought another, connecting, holding. Wyatt looked away first, shifting his gaze down, to the strings of his guitar.

Etta moved from her chair and joined Rachel on the ground. She lowered herself onto the blanket and reached for Kat.

"Let me help you with that little sweet thing." Etta held the child close. "I do love these babies."

"Me, too." Rachel exhaled and a chill swept up

her back. The night was getting cooler, the air was damp. The fire was burning out and the heat no longer reached where she sat.

"We should wrap this up." Jason Bradshaw put his drum down and looked around. The crowd had seriously disappeared. "Wow, where'd everyone go?"

"It's almost ten o'clock," Alyson informed him, smiling, her eyes revealing that she adored him.

"Wow." Jason leaned to kiss his wife.

Wyatt stood up, putting his guitar back in the case. He carried it to where she sat and leaned it against a chair. He towered over her and she breathed easier when he knelt next to them.

"Thank you for watching them for me."

Rachel held Molly close. "They were watching me."

"Let me get her and then I'll come back for Kat."

"I have an idea. You take her, I'll take Kat from Etta and carry her over for you."

He stared down at her and after a minute he nodded. But he had that look on his face, the same one as the other day when she'd opened the gate.

He took Molly from her arms, leaning in, his head close to Rachel's. She waited for him to move away before she stretched her legs and then stood. Etta smiled up at her, brows arching. But she didn't comment. Rachel loved that the other woman knew when to keep her thoughts to herself. Sometimes.

Rachel took Kat and held her in one arm. She extended her free hand and Etta took it, pulling herself to her feet.

"That ground isn't as soft as it used to be." Etta kissed Kat's cheek and hugged Rachel. "See you in a few days, Rachel Lynn."

"Let me know if you need me sooner."

"Will do, honey." And then Etta headed for Alyson.

Rachel headed toward the parking lot with Kat. When she reached Wyatt's truck Molly was already buckled in and his guitar case was in the front seat. He opened the driver's side back door and reached for Kat. His hands slid against Rachel's arms. He caught her gaze, held it for a second and then moved away.

Rachel backed up a few steps. "They're easy to love."

He smiled at that. "Yeah, they are."

She took another step back, trying not to think too much. He leaned against his truck, always the cowboy in his faded jeans and worn boots. He had on a ball cap tonight, though, no cowboy hat.

Time to make her escape.

"I'll see you in a few days." She backed up, tripping over the curb.

A hand shot out, grabbing her arm, steadying her. He laughed a little and winked. "You might want to work on that walking thing."

"Yeah, I might."

He let go of her arm. "Good night, Rachel."

She watched him drive away and then she hurried back to the leftover embers of the fire.

Chapter Five

Wyatt never would have imagined that one little pony would be so much trouble. But a few days after they brought Prince home, Wyatt was starting to see what he'd done. The night before, the girls had ridden the poor little animal until sunset. Wyatt had finally insisted they go inside and eat something quick before they crashed.

This day had been more of the same. The sun wasn't going down, but it was suppertime and the girls were hungry and beat. He wasn't too far behind them. Wyatt herded them into the laundry room, trying to ignore the massive pile of laundry that needed to be done. He kicked off his boots as the girls sat on the floor and pulled theirs off.

"What are we gonna eat?" Molly sat on the floor, her arms crossed over her raised knees. "Are you gonna cook?"

The cookbooks. He bent to help Kat get her left

boot off. Her cheeks were a little pink from the sun and her hair was tangled from the wind. They needed a bath and an early bedtime.

"I can try another recipe. I have hamburger."

Molly covered her face. "Not hamburgers."

Kat imitated her sister. "Not burgers."

"I don't mean hamburgers. I'll cook something *with* hamburger." He picked them up and walked into the kitchen. He put the girls down and Molly looked around, her face nearly as pink as her sister's. She opened the cabinet with cereal.

They'd had cereal the night before. And the night before that they'd eaten at the Mad Cow. He'd never been much of a cook. For the first year or so it hadn't seemed to matter. He'd been numb and food had just been food. Ryder had shaken him out of that way of thinking.

He really needed a housekeeper. He needed someone who could cook. He glanced at his girls sitting on the stools where they were waiting for him to cook something wonderful. Molly's braids were coming undone. She pulled it loose. They needed someone who could put ribbons in their hair.

Rachel Waters's image interrupted his thoughts and he pushed it aside as he reached into a drawer for the apron he'd bought a few days ago. He tied it around his waist and winked at his girls. They giggled and Kat covered her eyes.

Rachel Waters was not on the short list of people he could hire. He wasn't going to let her do this to him. She wasn't going to be traipsing around the place, smelling it up with her perfume, invading his peace and quiet.

"Okay, we need food."

"We need Rachel," Molly said, the voice of reason. He wasn't convinced. He had an apron. He could cook.

"Why do we need Rachel?" He stood next to his oldest daughter. Her arms wrapped around his waist and she held him close.

"She sings."

"Right, she sings." He didn't know if that qualified her to be their housekeeper. They needed a grandmotherly woman who knitted scarves. Yeah, that would be perfect.

"I'm hungry." Kat rubbed sleepy eyes with her pudgy fists.

"Right, and I'm cooking." Something quick and easy. He opened the casserole cookbook and found a recipe that included tater tots, soup and hamburger. Man, what could be easier than that?

Molly stared, her expression skeptical as he tossed the thawed hamburger into a heated pan and then turned on the oven to preheat. He glanced at the cookbook. To four hundred degrees.

"I can do this, Mol, I promise."

"Promise?" Kat covered her eyes again and peeked between her fingers.

"Kat, it isn't going to be that scary. Why don't you go wash up and it'll be ready soon."

Kat was drooping like some of the plants in the den. He guessed he had about ten minutes to get something in her before she crashed. They'd been having so much fun on the pony he hadn't paid attention to the time.

Eighteen long months of trying to make the right decisions. Eighteen months of wondering what he could have done to change the course of their lives. He should have noticed something that day when he left Wendy and the girls for a youth retreat.

He stirred the hamburger until it turned brown.

Instead of noticing the look in Wendy's eyes, he'd kissed her goodbye and wondered why she held him so long before he walked out the door. Even now, eighteen long months later, the memory shook him. He started to slam his fist into the wall, but the girls were there, watching. They kept him sane. They kept him being a dad and living his life.

They kept him in church when he would have

liked to walk away. They kept him from being so angry that he couldn't go on.

"Hey, you girls going to go clean up?"

He turned and Kat's head was on the granite top that covered the kitchen island. A chef's kitchen for a guy who could barely manage a bowl of cereal. Pretty crazy.

When he talked to the contractor last fall, he had this idea that a great kitchen would inspire him to cook. Instead, it inspired him to spend as much time as possible in the barn.

Molly stared up at him, her dark eyes seeing too much. She wasn't even four years old. She needed to chase butterflies and ride ponies, not spend her days worrying about her dad or what they'd feed her little sister. He hugged her.

"We can have cereal, Daddy," she whispered in his ear.

"No, we're not going to have cereal. We're going to have a casserole. Kat can nap while I cook." He glanced at the clock. It was almost seven. "Let's go wash your hands and I'll put your sister on the couch. We'll straighten up while the casserole cooks."

"You're a bad cleaner, Daddy." Molly leaned her head on his shoulder. "And you even burned our grilled cheese."

"I know, pumpkin, but tonight will be better. I have a cookbook."

Fifteen minutes later the smoke detector was going off and Kat was screaming the house down. He ran down the hall to grab a broom and he knocked the offending alarm off the ceiling. Smoke filled the kitchen and someone was banging on the back door.

Just what he needed. No reason to call and warn a person that you planned to visit.

"Come in." He could hear the girls crying. The upstairs smoke detector was now going off and the backdoor banged shut.

"Do I need to call the fire department?"

He was pouring baking soda on the flaming hamburger meat when his mother-in-law appeared at his side and sat a lid on the fiasco that was supposed to be dinner. His baking soda had already worked to put out the flames. He'd remembered that much from something he'd read years ago.

"Grandma." Molly and Kat in unison ran to Violet and hugged her legs. She hugged them back.

"Girls, get your shoes on, we're going to the Mad Cow." He ignored Violet and smiled at his daughters. And he hated ignoring Violet. She'd been more of a parent to him than the two he'd been stuck with at birth.

"This was their dinner?" Violet stood and flipped on the exhaust fan before opening the window over the sink. "Honestly, Wyatt, this isn't what I wanted to see when I showed up here."

"Well, Violet, I'm not sure what to tell you. Accidents happen."

"Of course they do."

Okay, so she was making him feel like a ten-year-old kid who had gotten caught writing on the bathroom wall. He jerked off the apron and tossed it on the counter. "Look, Violet, we're fine. The girls are fine."

"I know you're fine." She fiddled with the diamond rings on her left hand. "I'm not here to grade your progress. I'm here to see you."

"I didn't know you were going to be here today."

"I wanted to surprise the girls." Her arms were around his daughters again.

"I see." It felt like some kind of snap inspection.

"Let's take the girls to the diner and later we can talk."

"Talk about what, Violet?" He shot a look past her, to his daughters and he smiled a little softer smile. "You girls go find shoes and wash your hands and faces before we go."

Molly took Kat by the hand and led her out of the kitchen, down the hall. He could hear their little girl jabber and once they were out of earshot, he turned his attention back to Violet. He hadn't noticed before that she had dark circles under her eyes and more gray in her dark hair than the last time he'd seen her.

But then, he wasn't the most observant guy in the world.

"What is it we're going to talk about?" he reminded her when she didn't say anything.

"About the girls coming to spend time with me."

"Violet, I'll bring the girls to see you. Maybe in a week or two. We'll spend a couple of nights." He knew that wasn't what she wanted.

He pretended it was as he walked out the door to the laundry room and slid his feet into his boots. Violet followed him. She didn't belong here. She wore designer dresses and diamonds. Wendy had worn jeans and T-shirts.

A jacket on the hook next to his hat caught his attention. Not his jacket. He closed his eyes and remembered Rachel taking it off and hanging it there. Man, for a minute he almost felt at ease.

He glanced away, not wanting Violet to notice that jacket. It didn't mean anything, but it would imply a lot. He didn't want that hornet's nest opened, especially when there was nothing to know.

"You know that isn't what I mean. I don't want a day visit, Wyatt." Violet was a small woman with a will the size of Mount Rushmore. "I want to take the girls, maybe for the summer. I think you need time to get your head on straight. You can't do this, taking care of them, the house and the ranch, alone. I know you're trying, but you need help."

Anger simmered and he couldn't look at her. If his head hadn't been on straight, as she'd implied, he would have lost it right at that moment. He reached for his hat and shoved it down on his head. What he really wanted to do was walk out the door. If it hadn't been for his girls he might have.

"I'm together, Violet. I'm not a perfect parent. My cooking skills are pretty limited, but I'm doing what counts. I'm here every single day taking care of my girls. I'm the person making their breakfast and the guy who tucks them in at night."

Tears welled up in Violet's eyes. "I know you're a good dad. But I also think that maybe you're suffering and that isn't good for my granddaughters."

He turned away from his mother-in-law and rested a hand on the door, sucking in deep breaths, trying to keep it together before she had a real case against him.

"I'm not letting you take my girls."

"Wyatt, I didn't say I wanted to *take* them. I want to give you a break. Maybe you can find a housekeeper, someone to help with cooking and laundry? They're my granddaughters and I'm worried, that's all."

His daughters. He started to remind her of that fact, but footsteps in the hallway stopped him. He looked past Violet and smiled at Kat and Molly.

Molly's nose scrunched and her eyes narrowed as she looked from her father to her grandmother and he wondered how much she'd overheard, or if she'd heard any of it. Maybe she sensed the problem. Either way, he wasn't going to let her be a part of this.

Violet picked up her purse. She opened her mouth and he shot her a look that stopped her from saying more.

"Let's go, girls. We're going to the Mad Cow and I bet Vera will cook us up something special."

"Fried bologna sandwich?" Molly's eyes lit up and Violet gasped.

Wyatt picked up his two girls, one in each arm and walked through the back door, leaning against it to hold it open for his mother-in-law. She wasn't smiling and he didn't know if it was because she'd given up or was planning a new strategy. Maybe she was still trying to get over the idea of fried bologna?

A housekeeper, she'd said. As if he hadn't given it a lot of thought. But the one person that kept coming to mind was the last person he needed in his home on a daily basis.

Violet stood there for a moment, not walking through the door. He didn't have a clue what she expected from him. Maybe she wanted him to promise to send the girls with her, or maybe she expected him to cave on the subject of a housekeeper.

She walked out the door and he made the worst decision he figured he'd made in years.

"Okay, Violet, I'll hire a housekeeper." He let the door close and he followed her down the steps to her car. She'd won. He didn't know how, but he did know that this was a victory for his mother-in-law.

A warm breeze whipped the sheets on the clothesline. In the bright light of the full moon, Rachel unpinned the clothes she'd hung up earlier and pulled them down. She folded the crisp sheets, holding them to her face to breathe in the outdoor scent. They smelled like clover and fresh air.

The clip-clop of hooves on the paved road caught her attention. She looked into the dark and wondered who was lucky enough to be riding tonight. It was a beautiful evening with a clear sky and a light breeze that promised rain, but not yet.

She stood in the dark holding a pillow case she'd pulled down from the line and whispering for her dog to stay still. The German shepherd stayed at her side but he growled low, a warning for anyone who came too close.

The horse stopped and then the clip-clop continued. Instead of going down the road it was coming up the drive, hooves crunching on gravel. She grabbed the dog's collar.

"Laundry this late at night?" Wyatt's voice called from the dark shadows.

"Riding this late at night?"

He rode closer and the moonlight caught his face and the big gray that he rode. She shivered and felt the chill of the breeze against her arms.

"I had to get out of the house."

"Who's with the girls?" It came out like an accusation. She hadn't meant that. "I'm sorry, that's none of my business."

"No, it isn't." He sat steady on the horse that shifted a little and pawed the ground. "My mother-in-law."

"Oh, I see." But she didn't. She didn't know Wyatt, not really. She didn't know his life, other than caring about the girls and hearing about his wife's death. He didn't really share personal details.

She got that, because neither did she. Too many times in the past when she'd shared, it had been recycled and used against her.

"She showed up this evening." He swung down off the horse, landing lightly on the ground and holding the reins as he stood there.

Unsure. She was surprised to see him unsure. He should have looked confident standing there next to that horse. She wondered if it was about his mother-in-law. His hand went up, catching hold of the horse's bridle. The big animal pushed at his arm and Wyatt held him tight.

"I'm sure the girls are happy to see her." She held on to the laundry basket with one arm and with her left hand she kept hold of the dog that growled a low warning.

"They were. Unfortunately I was in the process of burning the house down when she showed up." Wyatt reached up and pulled something off his saddle. Her jacket that she'd left at his house. "I thought you might need this."

He dropped it in the laundry basket on top of the sheets she'd just folded. And then he stood there. She looked up, caught him watching her. It was hard to breathe when he did that.

"Would you like to go for a ride?" He said it so easy and nothing was that easy. No word fit him better than complicated. Everything about him fit into that box.

His mother-in-law was at his house and he was riding in the dark. That meant something other than "nice night for a ride."

But a moonlight ride with Wyatt Johnson seemed to trump the fear of complications and whatever was going on with him. Her gaze shifted to the tiny parsonage that she shared with her parents. Her mom was inside knitting. She'd had a rough day, a rough month. Rachel's dad was working on Sunday's sermon.

"We won't be gone long." Wyatt moved a little closer.

"I shouldn't. I have more laundry to do."

He laughed a little. "Are you always the good daughter?"

No, she wasn't.

Cynthia was the good one. That fact didn't hurt the way it once had. Life changed. Cynthia was married and had a family. Rachel lived with her parents, making sure their mother stayed healthy. It was an easy choice to make. Stay with her parents, help with their ministry and take care of them. Leaving wasn't an option, not when her brother and sister both lived on the other side of the country.

Her gaze landed on Wyatt's dusty boots and slid up. When she reached his face, he was smiling. And he winked. She nearly dropped the laundry basket and in her shock, she let go of the dog. Wolfgang jumped away from her. His tail wagged and he made a beeline for Wyatt.

"Hey now, you're a big old dog." His hand went out and the dog dropped on his belly. "And he's friendly."

"He isn't supposed to be."

"Oh, you want him to attack me?" Wyatt grinned again.

"No, but I don't want him to lose his edge. He's a guard dog."

"Right." Wyatt continued to rub the dog behind the ears. "So, you want to go? I can't be gone too long."

Rachel bit down on her bottom lip and then she nodded.

"Okay, let me take Wolfgang in and I'll put on boots."

"Flip-flops are okay."

"Right, so you can laugh at the city girl who wore the wrong shoes to go riding."

"Okay, I'll stand out here and hold on to Gatsby."

She laughed. "Gatsby."

"Oh, laughter from the woman with a dog named Wolfgang?"

She whistled and Wolfgang trotted to her side. "I'll be right back."

As she walked through the back door, letting it bang softly behind her, Rachel heard her dad on the phone. She glanced at the clock, surprised that he'd have a call this late at night. Hopefully no one was hurt or sick. Late calls were almost never a good thing. She peeked into the living room. Her mom was still sitting in the recliner next to the window, the lamp glowing soft light and her hands working the knitting needles as the scarf in her lap grew.

"Hey, I'm going riding with Wyatt Johnson." Rachel sat the basket of laundry on a chair and used what she hoped was a casual, it's-really-nothing voice.

Her mom glanced up. Gloria Waters always looked serene. Rachel envied that about her mother. She envied that her mom and sister could eat cake and never gain an ounce. And yeah, she knew that envy was wrong. But there were days she could really use a piece of cake.

Or maybe the whole cake. And that was the problem.

"Riding with Wyatt?" Gloria put her knitting down. "Okay, well, be careful."

What had she expected her mom to say? That she couldn't go? Rachel smiled. She was a dozen years past the time when her parents made decisions for her. And yet she still checked with them.

Her father's voice carried from his office. "I'm not sure if we're interested, Bill. I know we've talked about that. Let me pray on this…"

His voice faded. Rachel couldn't breathe for a second because she'd heard similar conversations in the past. She hadn't expected it now. She shifted her gaze to her mom and got a shrug, nothing more.

"What's going on?"

"I'm not sure. Your dad missed a call from Bill and he called him back."

Rachel nodded.

Her mom picked up her knitting again as if it didn't matter. Maybe it didn't. Maybe it was another door opening, another one closing. But she didn't want this door closed.

"I should go. Wyatt is waiting."

She walked out the back door still wearing her flip-flops. It wasn't cold but the air was damp and the breeze blew against her bare arms. She shrugged into the jacket that Wyatt had given her before she went inside.

"Ready to go?" Wyatt looked down at her feet. "I was kind of joking about shoes. Do you have boots?"

"I do. I'm sorry." She glanced back at the house.

"It isn't a big deal. You can wear those." His booted foot went into the stirrup and he swung into the saddle. He reached for her hand. "Come on."

She hesitated and then she grasped his hand. Strong fingers wrapped around hers. It felt like a lifeline.

Chapter Six

Wyatt grasped Rachel's hand and her fingers wrapped tight around his. It was easier to think about riding than to think about the lost look on her face when she walked out of the house. She had looked pretty close to shell-shocked.

"Put your foot in the stirrup." He moved his left foot and she slid her foot into the stirrup. "And up you go."

He pulled and she swung her right leg up and over, landing behind him. The horse sidestepped and then settled. Her foot was out of the stirrup. He slid his foot back into place and glanced back at her.

"Ready?"

She nodded but didn't say anything. Three minutes in the house shouldn't have done this to her. Maybe she'd had a day like his?

Gatsby headed down the road at an easy clip, his

gait smooth, his long stride eating up the ground and putting distance between them and the parsonage. Rachel was stiff behind him, holding the saddle rather than wrapping her arms around his waist.

"Where are we going?" Her voice trembled a little. She was close to his back but didn't touch him.

"Nowhere, just riding. I haven't done this in years. Since Violet is at the house I decided to get out and clear my head."

He was taking steps. The girls were with Violet. They were fine. He was fine. Rachel Waters was sitting behind him, and he thought he could hear a quiet sob as the horse's hooves pounded the pavement.

"We've got land down here. I'm going to cut across the field and hit a dirt road that will take us back to your place."

She didn't answer.

The gate was open and he rode Gatsby through the entrance. They hadn't put livestock on this place since last fall. The grass was growing up and in a month or so they'd cut it for hay.

The moon was almost full and the silver light that shone down on the field was bright. The grass blew and the moonlight caught the blades, turning them silvery green. Wyatt slowed the horse to an easy walk. Behind him, Rachel sighed. He hoped she'd relaxed a little.

They rode through the field. Wyatt felt the presence of the woman behind him, even though she hadn't touched him. He'd been impulsive in his life, but this one had him questioning what in the world he'd done. He'd planned on taking a ride and clearing his head. It wasn't often that he had a few minutes alone. Instead of being alone, he had Rachel Waters on the back of his horse.

Out of the corner of his eye he saw a flash of something running through the grass. The horse must have seen it at the same time. The animal jumped a little, knocking Rachel forward. Wyatt held the reins steady and tightened his legs around the animal's middle.

"Easy there, Gats. It's a nice night for a ride, but I'm not looking for a big run."

Rachel's arms were now tight around his waist. He smiled and remembered high school, pretending a car had died or run out of gas on a back road. He kind of figured he could spur Gatsby just little and send the animal running across the field, and keep Rachel Waters holding tight.

Instead he eased up on the reins but kept the horse at a steady walk. "He's fine, just startled. I think that was a coyote."

"I think so, too." Rachel's cheek brushed his

back and then was gone. But her hands were still at his waist.

"So what happened back at the house?" He eased into the conversation the same way he eased his way into the saddle of a green broke horse.

"Why don't you tell me what happened with your mother-in-law?"

He glanced back and then refocused on the trail that was overgrown from years of neglected riding. Rachel readjusted behind him. Her arms slipped from his middle and her hands grabbed the sides of his shirt.

"Okay, rock, paper, scissors." He turned sideways in the saddle and held his hand out.

She shook her head but she smiled and held her hand out.

"Fine. One, two, three." She cut his paper with scissors.

He groaned. "Me first. Great. My mother-in-law isn't positive I'm fit to be a parent right now."

She didn't respond.

"You still back there?" He glanced back, pushing his hat up a little to get a better look at the woman behind him.

"I'm here." And then a sweet pause with her hands on his waist. "She's wrong."

"Thanks." He spurred Gatsby a little and the

horse picked up his pace. "He'll be a good horse when we're done breaking him."

"Done breaking him!"

"Yeah, he hasn't ridden double before tonight. In a few weeks we're going to start him on roping."

"Great, I'm practice."

No, not practice, he wanted to tell her. But she was a soft, easy way to slip back into life. He hadn't thought about dating too much, about any other woman taking Wendy's place. It still wasn't the direction he planned to take, but life was pulling him back in.

"You're not practice. You're helping me." He assured her, smiling as the words slipped out, meaning more than she would understand.

"Oh, so I can add horse trainer to my résumé?"

That's right, they were talking about the horse being broke to ride double, not about his dating life.

"Yeah, and since I spilled it, I think it's your turn to talk."

No answer. They rode for a few minutes in total silence. No, not total silence, tree frogs sang and a few night birds screeched. Her arms slid around his waist again. Her chin brushed his shoulder.

"I really can't talk about it. It has to do with my dad and the church."

The years in Florida doing youth ministry

weren't that far behind him. He got that she couldn't talk. But whatever had happened, it'd upset her. He leaned back a little, turning his head. It caught him by surprise, that she was so close. His cheek brushed hers and she moved back.

A Justin McBride song filled the night air. Wyatt groaned and reached into his pocket for his phone. It was Violet. He answered and in the background he could hear Molly crying. He'd been wrong, to take off like this, to leave them.

"I'll be home in five minutes." He spoke softly to his mother-in-law, offered more assurances and slid the phone back into his pocket. "Mind going back to my place?"

She shook her head, but he wondered. If he was her, he'd probably mind. Man, even he wasn't crazy about going back. It wasn't about his girls. It was about not wanting to face Violet, not with Rachel on the back of his horse.

It took less than five minutes to get from the field to the dirt road and back to Wyatt's house. Rachel held tight as the horse covered the ground in an easy lope. She tried hard not to think about falling off at the pace they were going.

Falling off or facing Wyatt's mother-in-law? She had to wonder a little about which one would be worse. Falling off would leave more marks. She wasn't that stupid.

"You okay back there?" Wyatt's voice was raspy and way too sexy.

"I'm good." Ugh, she was horrible.

He chuckled, his sides vibrating under her arms. "Of course you are. I promise, Violet isn't dangerous. She's overprotective of the girls. I guess I am, too. Maybe that's why we clash on a regular basis."

"They're your girls, of course you're protective. I don't think you're over…" She sighed.

"I'm overprotective." He glanced back at her. "It's okay, I can handle it. There are reasons, Rachel."

"But sometimes…"

"No, not sometimes." He reined in the horse. "Okay, sometimes. I know Molly needs to be able to separate from me. The hour or so a week that she's in the nursery has helped."

"I can see that she's doing better." Without knowing all of the reasons why Molly was afraid, it was hard to help her.

She held on as he cut through a ditch and up the driveway to his house. It looked as if every light in the house was on.

Nerves twisted a funny dance in her stomach as he pulled the horse to a quick stop next to the back door. He didn't wait for her to slide off. Instead he swung his right leg over the horse's neck and jumped off, leaving her sitting on the back of the saddle.

The door opened as she was sliding forward into the saddle, grabbing the reins as the horse started to sidestep. He calmed the minute she held the reins. Wyatt took the steps two at a time and met his mother-in-law and Molly as they walked out the back door. Molly held her arms out to him, no longer crying, just sobbing and hiccupping a little into his shoulder.

"I'm here." He spoke softly to his daughter.

"She woke up and you were gone." Violet, a woman with soft features and hair that framed a face that was still young.

"I shouldn't have left."

His mother-in-law shook her head. "Wyatt, there are going to be times that you have to leave."

Rachel sat on the horse, waiting for them to remember her. She didn't want to be the witness to their pain. She didn't want to be the bystander who got in the way. Violet remembered her presence and turned to stare.

Emotions flickered across the woman's face. Anger, sorrow, it was difficult to tell exactly what Violet thought about Rachel's presence.

"I should go." She didn't really mean to say it

out loud. She slid to the ground, still holding the reins. "It isn't far. I can walk."

Wyatt, still holding Molly, came down the steps. "Don't be ridiculous. I'll drive you home, Rachel. Molly and I can drive you home."

"Rachel?" Violet walked to the edge of the porch. "Are you the Rachel that my granddaughters talk about nonstop?"

"I'm Rachel."

"Wyatt said you cleaned his home last week. Are you interested in the job on a permanent basis?"

Rachel shot Wyatt a look and she wondered if that was what this night ride had been about. Had his mother-in-law put him on the spot and he'd used Rachel as his get-out-of-jail card because she had cleaned one time?

"She makes the house smell good," said Molly, suddenly talkative. Rachel smiled at the little girl.

"Well, that sounds perfect to me." Violet smiled at her granddaughter. "Do you cook?"

Rachel nodded because she had no idea what to say. She avoided looking at Wyatt because he probably looked cornered. She knew that she felt pretty cornered. Cleaning Wyatt's house once did not make her a housekeeper and nanny.

"Perfect." Violet looked from Rachel to Wyatt. "When do you want her to start?"

"Violet, this is something Rachel and I need to discuss."

"Well, the two of you talk and I'll go check on Kat."

Rachel thought about reminding them that she was still there, still a grown-up who could make her own decisions, but the conversation ended and Violet went inside looking like a woman who had solved a national crisis.

"That went well." He walked down the steps, still holding Molly, toward Rachel. Wyatt took the leather reins from Rachel. "Let me unsaddle him and I'll drive you home."

"I can walk. Or call my dad." She hugged herself tight, holding her jacket closed against the sudden coolness in the wind.

Wyatt turned, pushing his hat back. He shook his head. "You aren't walking. You're not calling your dad. I'm driving you home. Right, Mol?"

Molly nodded against his shoulder. She looked so tiny in her pink pajamas and her dark hair tangled around her face. The security light caught her in its glow and her little eyes were open, a few stray tears still trickling down her cheeks.

"I'm sorry that Violet put you on the spot."

"I understand." She stepped closer. "Do you want me to take her while you unsaddle Gatsby?"

He dropped a kiss on his daughter's brow and nodded. Molly held out her arms. Rachel didn't know why it mattered so much to her, but it did. In her heart it mattered that this little girl would reach out to her. It changed everything.

It even changed that truck ride home, sitting with Molly between them and the stereo playing softly. It changed the way she felt when Wyatt said goodbye and then waited until she was in the house before he backed out of the driveway, the headlights flashing across the side of the house.

And then she refocused because her parents were still up, still discussing something that could change her life forever.

Wyatt turned up the radio as he headed down the drive and back to his house. Molly was in the seat next to him, curled over against his side. Her breathing had settled into a heavy pattern that meant she'd fallen back to sleep.

When he pulled up his driveway he could see Violet in the living room, watching for him to come back. His house. His life. His kids. Violet was their grandmother. As much as he cared for her, he didn't care for facing off with her tonight.

He definitely didn't like her trying to make decisions for him. Decisions such as hiring Rachel Waters to be his housekeeper. There were plenty of women out there who could do the job. Women with loose housedresses and heavy shoes. That seemed pretty close to perfect.

He stopped the truck and got out, lifting Molly into his arms and carrying her up the back steps. Violet met him. She pushed the door open and he stepped into the laundry room, kicking off his boots, still holding his daughter tight.

"You're dating her?" Violet followed him through the kitchen.

Man, he needed peace and quiet, not this. He needed to put his daughter to bed and think before he got hit with twenty questions. He wasn't dating.

He'd gone for a ride to clear his head and for whatever reason he'd let that ride take him straight to Rachel. It wasn't like he'd planned it.

"I'm going to put my daughter in bed, Violet."

He glanced back and she stood in the hallway, her eyes damp with tears but she wasn't angry. He let out a sigh and walked up the stairs to the room Molly and Kat shared. Twin beds painted white, pastel quilts with flowers and butterflies. It was the perfect room for little girls to grow up in. Until they started fighting like barn cats and needed their own space.

That wasn't something he wanted to think about, their growing up. He hoped they would always be close. He didn't want to think about them in their twenties, having one major fight and pulling away until...

He didn't want to go back and he wasn't going to let his girls be him and Ryder.

He put his daughter in her bed and pulled the quilt up to her chin. She opened her eyes and smiled softly, raising a hand to touch his cheek. Sleepy eyes drifted closed again and he kissed her cheek. "Love you, Molly."

"Love you, Daddy." She smiled but her eyes didn't open.

"I'm downstairs if you need me." He walked to the door. "I'm not going anywhere."

As he walked downstairs, he felt as if he was about to face the judge. Violet was waiting in the den. The TV was turned off. She put down her book, a book he knew she hadn't opened. He took off his hat and shoved a hand through his hair. And he stood there in the middle of the living room, unsure.

"What's going on, Wyatt?"

"There's nothing going on, Violet. I'm being a dad to my daughters and I'm raising horses with Ryder." He sat down on the couch and rubbed a hand over his face because he was a grown man and he really didn't feel the need to answer her questions. But he owed her something. "I'm not dating Rachel Waters. She's the pastor's daughter and she takes care of the girls when they're in the church nursery. She teaches their preschool Sunday school class."

"I see. Well, she's very pretty."

"Right." Was that a trick statement?

"Wyatt, someday you'll want to date again. You'll move on. That's okay."

He closed his eyes because it seemed like a real good way to avoid this discussion. Instead he got smacked upside the head with a vision of Rachel Waters. Facing Violet was easier than facing the image taunting him behind closed eyes.

Never in his wildest dreams would Violet have been the person telling him to move on.

"Hire her, Wyatt. She'd be perfect for the girls. They need someone like her in their lives."

"They have me." He twisted the gold band on his finger. Someday he would have to take it off. "No one can replace Wendy."

"She was my daughter, Wyatt. I think I know that no one can replace her. But I lost a husband once and I do know that we can't stop living."

"I haven't stopped living." Okay, maybe he had for a while.

He hadn't expected it to hurt when the grief started to fade and life started to feel like something he wanted to live again. Moving on felt like cheating.

"Wyatt, you're a good dad. You were a good husband."

He had wondered for a long time and never been able to ask if she blamed him. He sure blamed himself. He still couldn't ask.

"It's the hardest thing in the world, moving forward. But…" What else could he say? Moving forward meant accepting.

She leaned and patted his arm. "Don't beat yourself up too much for having good days."

She had lost her husband years ago. Wendy's dad had died at work. A sudden heart attack that took them all by surprise. A few years ago Violet had remarried. He admired her strength, even if she did try to run his life from time to time.

"If you don't hire Rachel, do you have any thoughts on who you would like to hire?" Violet picked up her purse and dug through it, pulling out a small tablet and pen.

"Someone capable." He pictured Rachel and brushed the thought aside to replace it with a more suitable image. "Someone older."

Violet laughed a little and wrote down something about unattractive older woman. Now she was starting to get it.

Chapter Seven

The new lambs frolicked next to their mothers. Rachel leaned against the fence and watched, smiling a little. And smiling wasn't the easiest thing to do, not after the previous evening's conversation with her parents.

This was her place, Dawson, this house and the sheep she raised. Working for Etta, that was another place where she fit. Finally, at twenty-nine she fit.

That meant something because growing up she'd been the misfit, the overweight rebel always compared to her older sister. Cynthia had been the pretty one, the good one. Rob, her older brother, had been the studious one.

Rachel had set out to prove that she had a mind of her own.

"Thinking?" Her dad appeared at her side.

She glanced at him, wondering when he'd gotten

those lines around his eyes and that gray in his hair. As a kid, she'd always imagined him young and capable. She'd never imagined her mother in bed for days, fighting a lupus flare-up that attacked her joints and caused fatigue that forced her to rest more often.

Parents weren't supposed to age.

"Yes, thinking."

"Rachel, if we get this church, you don't have to go."

She stepped back from the fence and turned to face him.

"If you go, I go."

"I know that's how you feel, but we also know how you feel about Dawson. In all of the years of moving, there's never been a town that became your home the way this town has. We want you to be happy."

"I'd be happy in Tulsa."

"No, you won't. But we will. We love the city and we need to live closer to the hospitals and doctors. We're not getting any younger."

She didn't want to have this conversation. She turned back to the small field with her six ewes and the three babies that had been born so far this spring.

"You're not old."

Her dad laughed. "No, we're not, but there are

things we need to consider. Promise me you'll pray about this. I don't want you to make this decision based on what you think we need."

"I'll pray." She sighed and rested her arms on the top of the gate. "When do they want you to take the church in Tulsa?"

"Six weeks. And remember, nothing is set in stone, not yet."

"But that isn't a lot of time for the church here to find a pastor."

"It isn't, but there are men here who should pray about stepping into the role. Sometimes God moves us so that others can move into the place where He wants them."

"True." She turned to face him. "But then I question why He brought us here just to move us."

"To everything there is a season, a purpose. God doesn't make mistakes, Rachel. If we're here for a year, there's a purpose in that year."

"I know you're right." She stepped away from the gate. "I have to run into town to get grain. Do you want lunch from the Mad Cow?"

"No, we're going to have sandwiches." He kissed the top of her head the way he'd done when she was a kid. He hadn't changed that much. He still wore dress slacks and a button-up shirt. He still parted his hair, though thinning, on the side.

He was still the person she turned to when she

needed advice. And sometimes she recognized that her parents were a crutch. They were her safe place. This was easier than getting hurt again.

She drove the truck to town. Not that she couldn't put feed in the back of her convertible, but she liked the old farm truck her dad had bought when they moved to Dawson. When she'd thought this would be the last move.

She'd been moving her entire life. From place to place, in and out of lives. She'd learned not to get too close. Either the friends would soon be gone, or they'd find out she was human, not at all the perfect preacher's kid.

But she was no longer a kid. And this time she'd gotten attached.

She parked in front of the black-and-white painted building that was the Mad Cow Café. It was early for the lunch crowd. That meant time to sit and talk to Vera, the owner. Maybe they could have a cup of coffee together.

A truck pulled in next to hers. She glanced quick to the right and nearly groaned. Wyatt Johnson in his big truck. He saluted with two fingers to his brow and grinned. That cowboy had more charm than was good for him.

Or anyone else, for that matter.

She guessed it would be pretty obvious if she backed out of her parking space and went on down the road, so she opened the door and grabbed her purse. Wyatt met her at the front of the truck. The girls weren't with him.

"How are you?" He pulled off the cowboy hat and ran a hand through hair that was a little too long. Dark and straight, it looked soft. She thought it probably was soft.

"I'm good. Where are the girls?"

"Andie and Ryder are home after a trip to the doctor in Tulsa. Andie is on the couch for the next month or so till the babies come, and she thought the girls could keep her entertained."

"That'll be good for all three of them."

"Yeah, it is."

"And your mother-in-law?" She walked next to him, his stride longer than her own.

"Interviewing housekeepers."

"Oh."

It shouldn't hurt, that he was going to pick someone else. Of course she didn't want a full-time job as anyone's housekeeper. She didn't even know that they'd be here for her to take such a job.

"It will make things easier," he explained it in a way that made her wonder if he wanted to convince himself.

"Of course it would."

"Do you have any suggestions?" He opened the door to the Mad Cow and she stepped in ahead of him, brushing past him, trying hard not to look at him, to look into those eyes of his, to not see the faded jeans, the scuffed boots or the buckle he'd won at Nationals back when he team roped. Before marriage, before horse training. He still roped in local events.

A few weeks ago she had watched from the bleachers. She had watched him smile and avoid the women who tried to get his attention. Those women rode horses and they understood his world.

She was still breaking in boots she'd bought when they moved to Dawson. And now she'd have to put them back in the closet like most forgotten dreams. She'd pack them up with childhood books, love letters she'd never sent and pictures of ranch houses she'd dreamed of owning.

Wyatt was a cowboy. He was the real deal. He even held the door open and pulled out a chair for her when Vera pointed them to a table in the corner.

And he did it because it was what men in Dawson did. It was the way they lived. Her heart ached clean through and she told herself it wasn't about him, it was about leaving.

"You know, I'm not used to seeing you without a smile on your face." He drew her back with that comment and she managed a smile. "Oh, that's not better."

She laughed. "Sorry, just a lot on my mind. What about Ernestine Douglas?"

"What? Ernestine's smile?"

She laughed at the pretend shock on his face. "As a housekeeper."

"I hadn't thought about her. Yeah, I might give her a call."

"She'd be great with the girls. Her kids are grown and gone."

Vera approached, dark hair shot through with silver, knotted at the back of her head and covered with a net. She wiped wet hands on her apron and pulled an order pad out of the pocket.

"What can I get you kids today?"

Wyatt laughed, "Vera, I wish I was still a kid. If I was twenty again I'd ride a few bulls and then take Rachel off to Tulsa for a wild night."

Vera tsk'd. "Wyatt Johnson, you're talking about our preacher's daughter. She teaches Sunday school and watches over your babies in the nursery."

"Yeah, but in this dream, we're still young and crazy. Remember?" Wyatt winked at Rachel and picked up the menu. "What's special today?"

Vera pointed at the white board on the wall near the register. "My special cashewed chicken, and the pile of nothing you're trying to feed us."

"Vera, Vera, I guess you won't give a guy a break."

"Not a chance."

He laughed and ordered the cashewed chicken. Rachel ordered a salad. But she wanted that cashewed chicken. She had always wanted what she shouldn't have, the things that weren't good for her. Fried chicken, chocolate and the cowboy sitting across from her. The last was new on the list of things she shouldn't want and couldn't have.

Wyatt watched Rachel pick at the salad she'd ordered. Lettuce with chopped-up turkey and ham and barely a dab of dressing. He felt kind of guilty digging into the plate of fried chicken chunks over rice that covered his plate, the special gravy oozed over the side and dripped onto the table. Cashews and chopped green onions topped it off.

The way he looked at it, skinny women ought to eat something fried every now and then. He grabbed the saucer from under her coffee cup and scraped some of his chicken onto it.

"What are you doing?" She put her fork down and wiped her mouth.

"Feeding you. If you haven't got the sense to eat some of Vera's cashewed chicken, I'm going to help you out."

"But I don't want it."

"Oh, yes, you do." He grinned, hoping she'd smile and look a little less cornered. Man, what was it about this woman? She didn't eat. She had a butterfly tattoo. She had secrets.

He had two little girls who needed him to stay focused.

He reached for his iced tea and the band on his left hand glinted, a reminder. And guilt. Because he still wore a ring that symbolized forever with a woman who was gone.

But her memory wasn't.

He sighed and Rachel lowered her fork. Her eyes were dark, soulful. She didn't smile but her eyes changed, softened. "You okay?"

"I'm fine. So, are you going to try the cashewed chicken?"

Rachel picked up her fork and took a bite. Her eyes closed and she nodded.

"It's as good as people say." Her eyes opened and she flashed him a smile. "And you Johnson boys are as wicked as they say."

"We're not really wicked." He wanted to hug her tight because she was dragging him past a hard place in his life and she didn't even know it. "We're just on the edge a lot of the time."

"Temptation."

"Reformed."

The door opened. The lunch crowd was piling

in. While they'd been talking the parking lot had filled up with farm trucks, a tractor or two and a few cars. He knew about everyone in Dawson and he figured Rachel did as well.

"We're about to get caught."

Rachel shrugged, "Yeah, that's life in Dawson. I love it here."

She sounded as if that meant something.

"You know, if you need to talk, I know how to keep a secret."

Her smile was sweet. She wasn't a girl from Dawson, but she fit this place, this world. From her T-shirt to her jeans, she was fitting in. But maybe that's what she did. The life of a preacher's kid wasn't easy. They moved a lot, changed towns, changed schools and changed friends.

Maybe she knew how to become the person each town or church expected her to be? Did that mean she wasn't who he thought she was? That left him kind of unsettled.

"I need to go. I don't want to leave the girls too long. They…" He stood up and dropped a few bills on the table for their lunch and Vera's tip. "The girls worry if I'm gone too long."

Rachel stood up. "Wyatt, if you need anything, I'm here."

Man, he could think of a list of things he needed.

He needed to keep his life together. He took a step back. He really wasn't ready for this.

The Johnson brothers weren't the only temptation in town.

Trouble was looking him in the eyes and it was about time he made the great escape. He and Ryder had done a lot of that in their younger days. They had experience. They knew how to race through a hay field to escape an angry dad. They knew how to escape the county deputy on a dirt road. Not exactly life lessons he was proud of.

He touched the brim of his hat. "Thanks for recommending someone. I'll call Mrs. Douglas."

"Right, that's a good idea."

"Or you could take the job? The girls would love that."

"I don't think so."

"Yeah, of course."

He bumped into a chair as he backed away from her and a few of the guys called out names and other things he didn't really want to deal with.

The only good idea right now was to escape Rachel Waters, maybe spend some time at Ryder's knocking the tar out of the punching bag still hanging in the old hay barn. Their dad had put that thing up years ago. He had taught them one decent lesson in life, other than how to make money. He'd taught them the art of boxing.

And right now felt like a pretty good time to go take a few swings at an inanimate object.

There were a list of reasons why. Wendy's memory, tugging him back in time and pushing him to think about how he'd let her down. His girls hurting and needing their mom. Rachel Waters with brown eyes and a butterfly tattoo, offering to be there for him but rejecting a job offer to take care of his girls.

Thoughts of Rachel felt a lot like cheating.

Thirty minutes after he left the Mad Cow he was in the barn behind Ryder's house. He had spent fifteen minutes in that hot, dusty barn slamming his fists into the frayed and faded bag that hung from the rafters.

"Trying to hurt someone?"

Wyatt punched the bag and then grabbed it to keep it from swinging back at him. He turned, swiping his arm across his brow. Boxing in boots and jeans, not the most effective form in the world.

Ryder stood in the doorway, sunlight behind him. They'd taken a few swings at each other over the years. The last time had been about something crazy, a woman that Ryder had hurt. It shouldn't have mattered to Wyatt—he hadn't known her. But Ryder had left a trail of broken hearts in his reckless wake.

They hadn't talked for over a year after that fight.

"No, just exercising." Wyatt stepped away from the punching bag.

Ryder grinned and shook his head. "Right, and that's why you were in town having lunch with Rachel Waters."

"That's why I don't like this town." Wyatt walked past Ryder, into the warm sunlight. At least there was a breeze. He didn't put his hat back on but stood there for a minute, cooling down.

"Yeah, people talk. Most of the time they're talking about me. Or at least they used to. Kind of nice to have you being the target of the gossip."

Wyatt walked on, toward his truck. "How's Andie?"

"Itching to get out of bed. The church brought a truckload of frozen meals for us and a few of the ladies cleaned the house. Rachel came over yesterday and brought a pie."

"Of course she did."

"Want a glass of tea or a bottle of water?" Ryder had stopped and that forced Wyatt to stop and turn around.

"Nope, I need to get home to the girls. Violet is trying to find a housekeeper-slash-nanny for us. I'm leaving it up to her, but I want to keep an eye on things."

"Wyatt, I know you're still angry or hurt. I know this messed you up, but it's time…"

Wyatt took a step in Ryder's direction. "Don't tell me when it's time, little brother. You think because you're married and finally getting it together, you have it all figured out. You don't have a clue how I feel."

Man, *he* didn't even know how he felt. So being angry with Ryder, wanting to shove him into the dirt, probably wasn't the right reaction. He sighed and took a step back, tipping his hat to shade his face.

"I'm sorry, Ryder. But let me figure this out, if you don't mind."

"Got it. But I wanted you to know," Ryder looked down and turned a little red. "We're praying for you."

That was a change for his brother. Ryder was now the one with the stronger faith. That was another thing Wyatt was working on getting back. He'd walked away from the ministry and spent a long year blaming God. He'd spent the last six months working through that and trying to find peace.

"Ryder, I appreciate that."

Ryder grinned. "Yeah, do you appreciate how hard it was to say?"

They both laughed.

"Yeah, cowboys from Dawson don't have a lot of Dr. Phil moments."

"Ain't that just about the truth?" Ryder slapped him on the back. "See you later. If I don't get in there, she'll be climbing the curtains."

Wyatt watched his brother walk away and then he headed for his truck. He sat behind the wheel for a minute, letting things settle inside him and watching as Rachel Waters jogged down the driveway and away from his house.

Now what in the world was that all about?

Chapter Eight

Friday night lights had a different meaning in Dawson, Oklahoma, than it did in Texas. Friday nights in Dawson meant the local rodeo at the community arena. Trucks and trailers were scattered in the field that served as a parking lot and cars parked in the small lot that used to be gravel, but the rain had washed it out last fall and so now it was dirt, grass and some gravel.

Wyatt's truck and trailer were parked near the pens where livestock were ready for action. There were a half-dozen bulls, a small pen of steers and a few rangy horses. Someone had dropped off a few sheep for the kids' mutton bustin' event.

The youth group from Community Church was busy cooking hamburgers on a grill as a fundraiser for their trip to Mexico. Pastor Waters had asked him to think about going as a counselor. He wasn't ready for that but he'd agreed to pray.

Maybe soon, though.

He watched the crowds file in, taking seats on the old wooden bleachers. His girls were with Violet. She should be there by now. She'd stayed at home to make more calls to prospective house-keepers. He had thought about stopping her. He had managed just fine all this time, so why did he need someone now?

He wasn't sure he liked the idea of a stranger in his home, taking care of his kids, cooking their meals. The one thing about Violet, she was deter-mined. She'd informed him she had one woman that seemed to be perfect for the job. Great.

"Hey, are you competing tonight?" Ryder walked through the pen of steers, his jeans tucked into boots that were already caked with mud.

The rain they'd had that morning had cooled the air and left the arena pretty soupy. It had also brought a lot of rocks to the surface inside the arena.

"I'm going to rope with Clint Cameron. How's Andie?"

Ryder shuddered. "Not a good patient. You know she doesn't like to sit still. But she'll do it for the girls. Etta is with her tonight."

Twins. Wyatt shook his head and laughed a little. In less than a month his brother was going to be daddy to not one, but two babies. It had taken Andie and those babies to settle Ryder.

"She'll survive it. I'm not sure about you." Wyatt slapped his brother on the back. "You getting on a bull tonight?"

"Andie said if I get on a bull and break my leg, she'll break my neck. Think she means it?"

"Yeah, she probably does."

He glanced toward the bleachers again, looking for his girls. He spotted Violet, but not the girls. He scanned the area around her and didn't see Molly or Kat. Ryder was still talking, but Wyatt held up a hand to stop him.

"I have to go find the girls."

"Aren't they with Violet?"

"They were supposed to be." Wyatt stepped around his brother. "I'll be back."

"Do you want me to help you look?"

"No, I've got it. You stay here in case they show up over here. Maybe they gave her the slip."

He walked on the outside of the arena, ignoring a few people who called out to him and sidestepping puddles left behind by the downpour.

A child yelled. He glanced toward the refreshment stand and his heart hammered hard. Molly and Kat, each holding a corn dog. And Rachel Waters standing next to them. He stopped and then moved quick to get out of the way of a few riders about to enter the arena for the opening ceremony.

The horses moved past him and he had to search again for Rachel and the girls. They were standing a short distance away. Molly laughed and Rachel wiped her cheek. Kat was shoving fries in her mouth. Ketchup had dripped down the front of her plaid shirt and her jeans had dirt on the knees. Her pink boots were almost brown from dirt and mud. His little girl.

Rachel looked up and her smile froze when she saw him. He headed in their direction with anger and some other emotion having a doggone war inside him. Why were his girls with Rachel, not Violet?

Man, seeing her with his girls, seeing them smile like that. Come to think of it, he wasn't even sure he was angry, just confused.

"You have my girls." He spoke as softly as he could, not raising his voice, but it wasn't like he was happy.

"I do." Rachel touched each of their heads. She wasn't eating a corn dog. "I pulled in right after they did. When we got inside the gate, the girls asked Violet for something to eat. I was heading this way, so I told her I'd get them something. Is that okay?"

"Of course it is." He said the words like it was easy and didn't matter.

Rachel remained a few feet away, shifting back and forth on city-girl boots, her jeans a little too long. Her T-shirt said something about joy. A few curls sprang rebelliously from the clip that held her hair in a ponytail.

"I'll take them back to Violet."

"Let them finish eating and I'll take them back with me. They want to see the calves and the sheep."

"Okay." She bent and dropped a kiss on the top of Molly's head and then she hugged Kat. "I'll see you later."

"Why don't you come with us? I'll show you the horse I traded for this morning." He didn't know if she cared about a horse. But he did know that he wanted to keep his daughters smiling.

And the smile he got in return, her smile, kind of shattered his world a little. It also made him regret not thinking this through more carefully.

The girls finished their corn dogs and tossed the sticks in the trash. Rachel wiped their hands with a napkin and then their mouths. Wyatt stood back, like a bystander, observing. She made it all look so easy.

But nothing was simple, not even the way she

twisted his emotions. She had somehow hijacked his life and he didn't think she even knew it.

"Let's go." She smiled at him, her hands holding tight to Kat and Molly.

The girls led Rachel as they followed Wyatt back to pens on the north side of the arena. Cattle mooed low and a few sheep bleated their dislike of the muddy pens. A horse whinnied and someone laughed loud. Rachel followed that sound to the source.

The source happened to be tall and wiry with sandy brown hair that curled just a little and a big smile that flashed in a suntanned face. Black framed glasses somehow made his angular features look studious.

He was one of the Cooper brothers, she couldn't remember which. It surprised her to see him at a local event. He was a bullfighter for the professional bull riding events across the country. Tall and wiry, he made his living jumping in front of bulls and taking the shots to keep the bull riders safe.

She knew a daredevil when she saw one. And a flirt.

He lived up to his reputation, jumping one of the fences to land in front of her. Wyatt turned, his smile dissolving when the unknown Cooper took off his hat and bowed in front of her.

"Pleasure to meet you, ma'am." His accent was a little heavy. Andie had told her that she thought he used his Russian heritage to woo the ladies and that his accent hadn't been as heavy a few years back.

She smiled because he was cute and she wasn't interested.

Wyatt appeared at her side. She shivered a little because he didn't appear to be in a great mood. Nor did he appear to be too patient.

"See you later, Travis." He nodded curtly.

The younger man laughed and mumbled something about striking out before he climbed back over the fence to finish saddling his horse.

"He's always up to something." Wyatt led them through a crowd of men and then to his truck and trailer. A pretty chestnut, deep red with white socks, was tied to the back of his trailer.

"He's beautiful." Rachel ran a hand down the horse's sleek neck.

"I thought so. I bought him at the auction the other night. People are dumping horses like crazy."

"I heard that they're being abandoned on government land."

Wyatt nodded. "This guy belonged to some

folks over by Grove. They had to sell all of their livestock."

"I had planned on getting a horse." She stroked the fine boned face of the gelding. His ears pricked forward and he moved to push his head against her arm.

"Planned. You still could. If you decide to get one, I can take you to the auction and we can find you a good deal."

"Thanks, but…" She sighed and focused on the horse, much easier than looking at the cowboy leaning against the horse's saddle where he'd placed his two little girls. His arm was around Molly's back, holding her in place.

"But?"

"But I think right now isn't the right time for me to buy a horse." She smiled and pretended it didn't hurt. "I should go. Do you want me to take the girls back to Violet?"

"First name basis with my mother-in-law?"

"She took me to lunch today." She admitted with a fading sense of ease.

"That's great. Well, I do love to know that my life is being arranged for me." He lifted the girls down and then he put them in the back of his truck. "Stay there and don't get down. There are too many hooves back here and not enough people paying attention."

When he headed her way, Rachel shivered a little. She'd seen that stormy look on his face before. His dark eyes pinned her to the spot where she stood. He untied his horse, still staring at her.

"Rachel, I take care of my girls. I might not be the best cook in the world and maybe my house gets messy, but I haven't let them down. I hope you know that."

"Of course I do." She wanted to touch his arm, to let him know that she wasn't the enemy. She kept her hands to herself. "Violet knows you're a good dad. She's only trying to help. Maybe it's misguided, but…"

"I get that." He led the horse away from her. "I have to get in the arena to ride pickup. Can you take the girls back to Violet?"

"I can. And for what it's worth, I'm sorry."

He tipped his hat and rode off, the horse splattering mud as his big hooves bit into the ground. She stood there for a minute and then she turned to the girls. They were sitting on the tailgate of the truck, waiting. They knew better than to get down. She smiled at them and the two smiled back. They looked sweet in their plaid shirts, jeans and little boots.

Violet must have dressed them. She smiled and reached for their hands. "Let's head back to Grandma and watch the rodeo."

Rachel led the girls back through the crowd of cowboys. A few were zipping up their Kevlar vests in preparation for the bull rides. Bulls moved through the pens and a couple of the big animals were being run into chutes.

Adam MacKenzie stood next to Jason Bradshaw. They were watching one of the bulls, a big gray animal that snorted and when he shook his head, he sent a spray of slime flying through the air.

Kat giggled and wiped her cheek.

"Hey, girls." Jason lifted his hand and Molly high-fived him. "You having fun with Miss Rachel?"

Kat nodded big and smiled. "She could live with us."

Heat crawled up Rachel's cheeks. Jason and Adam laughed but they were definitely curious, she could see it in widened eyes and raised brows.

"Wyatt is thinking about hiring a housekeeper," she explained. "I'm *not* applying for the job."

"Oh, then that makes perfect sense." Jason was married to Etta's granddaughter, Alyson. Ryder's wife Andie was Alyson's twin.

Rachel smiled at Jason and kept walking, a little girl on each side of her.

A person didn't have to go far in Dawson to find people who were somehow related. Andie had told her it made dating in Dawson a real challenge.

The reason Andie had explained that to her was because she wanted Rachel to know that she shouldn't have a difficult time finding someone to date in Dawson. At least she wasn't anyone's cousin.

At the time it had been funny. Now, not so much. If the church in Tulsa called, she would be gone by the end of June. Once again she had been smart not to get too attached.

Of course, she was just lying to herself. The two little girls holding her hands as they headed for the bleachers happened to be proof that she had gotten attached. The fast beating of her heart when she turned to watch Wyatt rope a bull that refused to leave the arena could probably be called serious evidence.

When they reached Violet, she smiled at the girls and patted the bench next to her. "Come on, girls, time to sit and watch."

A rider was already flying out of the gate on the back of a big white bull. The ride didn't last three seconds. The bull twisted in a funny arc, jumped and spun back in the other direction. Rachel held her breath as the rider flew through the air and landed hard on his back.

"Who was that?" Rachel leaned to ask Jenna who sat on the bench in front of her.

"I think it was one of the Coopers. I can't keep them all straight."

It must have been because Travis Cooper hopped in front of the bull, distracting it while Jackson ran through the gate to the fallen rider. Rachel bit her lip hard and watched, waiting for the rider to move, waiting as the medics hurried into the arena.

A leg moved, then an arm. The cowboy sat up. Rachel released her breath. The crowd erupted in applause. The cowboy lifted his hat as he stood, but then he went limp and his brothers lifted him and carried him from the arena.

"I have a love–hate relationship with this sport," Jenna MacKenzie said. She looked back and shook her head as she made the quiet comment. "I know why they do it. And then I wonder why they do it."

Rachel's gaze traveled to the back of the arena, to the rider holding his horse back from the fray, waiting for the next rider out of the chute. His rope was coiled, ready in case of emergency. He was all cowboy in a white hat, his button-up shirt a deep blue. She remembered the silver cross dangling from a chain around his neck.

If she didn't care, it wouldn't hurt to leave.

But she did care. Kat cuddled close, leaning and then curling on the bench to rest her head on Rachel's lap. Violet handed her a blanket. Kat carried that blanket everywhere, even to the nursery on Sunday.

Rachel dropped it over the little girl who dozed, thumb in her mouth. Molly was still bright-eyed, watching another bull being loaded into the chute. A rider on the catwalk prepared to settle himself on the animal's back.

But it all lost importance because Kat was curled next to her asleep. Rachel stroked the child's hair and Kat cuddled closer. By the time saddle broncs were run into the chutes for that event, Kat had climbed into her arms.

Nothing had ever felt as sweet, or hurt so much. It reminded her of waking up with the tail end of a wonderful dream still fresh on her mind and realizing it had just been a dream.

The cowboy who owned that dream was on his horse, taking the part of pickup man for the saddle bronc event. He glanced up at them, nodding and touching the brim of his hat. Molly waved big. He waved back, grinning. Oh, that grin. In his dark tanned face it flashed white and crinkled at the corners of his eyes. She didn't have to see the details because it had been imprinted in her mind.

His gaze settled on Rachel and Kat. She smiled and nodded. But then his attention returned to the task at hand.

Tension knotted in Rachel's lower back. Maybe due to the child in her arms, having to sit so straight, or the stress of watching men take risks on wild animals. Or maybe because Wyatt Johnson unraveled her a little, making her feel undone and kind of crazy.

She tried to remember the last time a man had made her feel that way. It had to have been when she was fourteen and Andy Banks was the star football player who lived next door. He had been nice when they walked to school together. But one day she'd heard him in the hall talking about her weight and how he thought she had a crush on him. It had turned into a big joke for him, something to laugh about behind her back.

It no longer hurt, but it was something she still remembered. That kind of pain left a scar.

It made it hard to believe in a smile.

But that girl was long gone. That girl had learned to eat healthy and exercise. After losing fifty pounds she'd seen Andy again and he hadn't recognized her. He'd actually smiled and flirted.

Rachel pushed back against those old feelings because she was the person God had created her to be. Fat or skinny, she was His. She knew who she was, and where she was going. She wasn't the person those kids had teased or the girl who had rebelled trying to find herself.

Instead she was the person who had taken control of her life. She had started believing in herself, who she knew she was and stopped believing the lies that were whispered behind her back.

Jenna reached back and touched her hand. "Wyatt's sweet."

Rachel nodded but she didn't know what to say, not when her own thoughts were still in a chaotic jumble and his mother-in-law had just left for a few minutes to stretch her legs.

"Yes, he really loves his girls."

Jenna laughed a little, "Okay, sure, that's what I meant."

Rachel knew what Jenna meant but she didn't comment. Instead she watched Wyatt ready his horse to run it up alongside the saddle bronc as the cowboy on the bucking animal made a leap and landed on the back of the pretty chestnut gelding Wyatt had bought at the auction. The cowboy immediately slid to the ground and headed back to the gate as the judge called out his score.

She was way too old for crushes. When Violet returned, Rachel made up an excuse why she had to leave. It wasn't really an excuse. She had a lot to do tomorrow and she didn't want to get to bed too late.

She kissed the girls goodbye and eased down the bleachers to the ground. Wyatt turned, nodding when he saw her on the grassy area next to the arena. She smiled back, trying to pretend the moment meant nothing to her.

The choir had taken their seats when Wyatt walked through the back doors of the church Sunday and found a seat near the front of the sanctuary. He'd taken the girls from the preschool Sunday school class to the preschool nursery. No Rachel in nursery this morning. His gaze scanned the front of the church, remembering she was in the choir.

She had taken her seat on the left side of the stage with the other altos. Her choir robe was red and white. She stood as the song leader hurried onto the stage. Her hands were already clapping the beat of a fast-paced song. As he stood there like an idiot, her gaze shifted. She smiled big and waved a little.

He hadn't felt so completely tongue-tied since seventh grade and Cora Mason, a ninth grader, had thought he was pretty cute. She had teased him for a couple of weeks and then informed him that he was too young. He wasn't twelve anymore.

And the preacher's daughter wasn't too old for him or a flirt. She laughed and sang a song about joy. He had to refocus, from Rachel to the music.

The music invaded his spirit, pushing the darkness from the corners of his soul.

It was easy to find faith here. This church, Pastor Waters, it all worked together to make a difference in a heart that had been ready to turn itself off to anything other than anger and bitterness. There were moments when he started to feel alive again, as if he could turn it all around. He had been thinking about the teens in this church, not having a youth leader. Everyone scrambled to find activities that kept them out of trouble and gave them options on weekends when there wasn't much to do in Dawson other than get in trouble.

As the choir switched to a more worshipful song, Wyatt closed his eyes. He sang along, listening for one voice. But another spoke to his heart, this one said to trust.

When he opened his eyes the choir was walking off the stage. Rachel hurried out the side door. He smiled because he knew that she would be going back to the nursery. No one could ever accuse of her of sitting by, waiting for someone else to do the work.

Her mother, often fighting sickness, sat behind the piano. She had days when she couldn't make it to church, but when she did make it, she played the piano and taught a Sunday school class.

People made choices every day, how to deal with

pain, what to do with anger. He remembered back to being a kid in church and the anger over his dad's affairs. He had been angry when the affairs were made public, but he hadn't blamed God. He'd blamed the person responsible, his father. Ryder had blamed God.

Eighteen months ago, Wyatt had been the one blaming God.

He leaned back in the pew and listened to the sermon. It took concentration to hear the words, but as he listened something in that sermon sounded like goodbye. It had to be his imagination. By the time the sermon ended, he was sure of it. It was just a sermon about moving on in life, making choices, following God. That wasn't a goodbye.

The congregation wasn't in a hurry to leave, but Wyatt had two girls waiting to be picked up from the nursery. He shook a few hands and moved past a crowd that seemed like it might pull him into a long conversation. When he reached the back door, Pastor Waters stopped him.

"No church tonight, Wyatt, but I wanted to talk to you if you have time."

"This evening?"

"If that's okay."

Wyatt glanced at his watch. Violet had stayed home to fix a roast and he had a horse that needed one more day under the saddle before his owner picked him up.

"Seven o'clock okay?"

Pastor Waters nodded. "Sounds good. I'll meet you here."

"Good. I'd better get my kids."

Wyatt hurried down the hall to the nursery. He peeked in and his girls were the last to be picked up. Rachel leaned to tie Molly's shoes. Wyatt waited, not saying anything. He watched as she made the loop and then hugged his little girl. Kat turned and saw him.

"Daddy!"

"Hey, kiddo." He leaned over the half door and picked her up. Little arms wrapped tight around his neck. "Did you have fun?"

Kat nodded, "We made Nose Ark."

"Noah's ark! Cool beans!"

"And there were lions and they roared," Kat continued. "And fish."

"Fish on the ark?"

Kat nodded, pretty serious about the whole thing. "And Rachel said we could fish."

He glanced over his daughter's head and made eye contact with Rachel. She bit down on her bottom lip and shrugged a little. Nice way to look innocent.

Chapter Nine

Rachel smiled at Molly. The little girl stood next to her, looking first to Wyatt and then back to Rachel, her eyes big. Rachel smiled at Wyatt, too, ignoring that he looked a little put out. "You can go, too."

"Where are you going fishing?" He leaned against the door frame, still holding Kat.

She knew this had to be difficult. For the last six months he'd kept them pretty close. Now Violet was pushing him to get a housekeeper and Rachel wanted to take them off fishing.

"To the lake. I have permission to fish off a dock that belongs to one of our church members. It's a pretty day and…"

She was rambling. He did that to her, and she really resented that he managed to undo her ability to hold it together. He was just a man. A man in jeans, a dark blue polo and boots. His hair was brushed back from his face, probably with his hand. And he'd shaved for once. His cologne drifted into her space, a fresh, outdoorsy scent.

Right, just a man.

So why couldn't she focus and act like the adult she was? He was leaning, hip against the door frame, watching her, his dark eyes a little wicked, sparkling with something mischievous; as if he knew that she wanted to step closer.

One of the Sunday school teachers appeared behind him, opening her mouth to say something. Maria, just a few years older than Rachel, looked from Wyatt to Rachel and then she scurried away mumbling that she'd catch up with her later. That left her, Rachel, stuck in a quagmire of emotion she hadn't been expecting.

She climbed out of the emotional quicksand and got it together.

"If it isn't a good day…" She had been so sure of herself that morning when the idea hit.

So much for the butterfly on her back serving as a reminder to think before acting. If she'd followed that rule she would have allowed him to sign his girls out, and she'd have driven on to the lake alone. Alone was much less complicated than this moment with Wyatt.

"It actually is a good day." He glanced out the window, and she followed his gaze to blue skies and perfectly green grass. "It's a perfect day. I have a young horse that I need to work before his owner picks him up. I think Violet is leaving so it would be good to work him without the possibility of little girls racing across the yard."

"Good, then this works for both of us." She felt a funny sensation in her stomach. "I'll pack a lunch and we'll make a day of it."

"Is it Frank Rogers's dock?"

"It is."

"Good, I just like to know where they are."

"We can go?" Molly jumped up and down. "And take our swimsuits?"

"If your daddy says it is okay. I'll go to our house and make sandwiches while you take them home to get play clothes. Swimsuits, if you don't mind them getting in the water."

"If you keep them in the shallow water."

"I think we can manage." She watched him leave with the girls and then she packed up her bag and headed out. This felt good, spending time with the girls. She had wanted to do it since they showed up in Dawson, but up till now he hadn't looked as if he would agree to let them go.

But today she would teach them to fish. And she wouldn't think about not being here at the end of the summer.

Two hours later, although fishing was her plan, she realized fishing was the last thing the girls wanted. Try as she might, Rachel couldn't get them settled down next to her on the dock's wooden bench. Instead they were running back and forth, sticking their feet in the water.

Kat wrestled with her life jacket, wishing, over and over again, that she could take it off. Finally she sat down next to Rachel, her little head hanging as she fiddled with the zipper.

"Leave it on, Kat." Molly lectured in a voice far older than a three-, almost four-year-old.

"I'm big enough."

Rachel smiled and shook her head at the statement.

"I tell you what, girls, let's skip rocks. And maybe we can wade." She looked around, spotting the perfect way to kill time. "Or we could take a ride on the paddleboat!"

Both girls let out squeals of delight. Who needed to catch fish, when there was something as fun as a paddle boat? She tightened the life jacket that Kat had managed to loosen and lifted her into the boat. Molly went in the seat next to her. Rachel untied the fiberglass boat and settled into the empty seat next to the girls. She started to peddle and the little boat slid away from the dock.

Waves rolled across the surface of the lake making it rough going for one person pedaling against the wind. But the girls didn't mind. Rachel looked down at the two little girls, their faces up to the sun and eyes closed against the breeze.

They were quite a distance from shore when she turned and headed them back toward the dock. Kat leaned against her, groggy, her thumb in her mouth. Rachel leaned back, her arms relaxed behind the two little girls.

It was moments like this she ached for a child of her own. She wanted to be someone's wife, the mother of their children.

A few years ago she had started to doubt that dream.

Her sister, Cynthia, had chided her for martyrdom. She said Rachel was giving up her life to take care of their parents. Rachel shrugged off that accusation. It wasn't martyrdom, not really. It wasn't even guilt, not anymore. It had started out that way, but over the years, when no handsome prince appeared, she stopped believing that there would be one for her.

Cynthia had a house in the suburbs. Rachel had boxes that she kept in the closet for the next move.

She didn't want to think about moving again, not now with the girls next to her. If they moved, it would hurt in a way that no move had ever hurt before. She leaned to kiss Kat on the top of her head.

Time to push these thoughts from her mind and enjoy this day. She didn't know for certain that her dad would take a new church. He never made a decision without prayer. And Rachel was praying, too. Because she didn't want to leave Dawson.

The horse stood stiff-legged with Wyatt in the saddle. He really didn't want to get thrown today. He should have stopped when he finished working the other horse, but this one couldn't be put off. He gave the horse a nudge with his heels. The leather of the saddle creaked a little as the horse shifted. Wyatt settled into the saddle and the gelding took a few steps forward. He pushed his hat down a little because he wasn't about to lose a brand-new hat.

A car pulled up the drive and honked. Great.

The horse let loose, bucking across the arena, jerking him forward and then back. Wyatt tightened his legs around the horse's middle and held tight. Man, he really didn't like a horse that bucked.

Eventually the animal settled and Wyatt held him tight. The horse stood in the center of the arena, trembling a little and heaving.

"Sorry, Buddy, I'm still back here. You aren't

my first trip to the rodeo." He nudged the horse forward and they walked around the arena.

They did a few laps around the arena, the horse jarring him with a gait somewhere between a walk and trot. Wyatt nodded when his mother-in-law approached the fence. He'd thank her later for the ride he hadn't really wanted to take.

At least the horse had calmed down and they would end this training session with the gelding remembering that Wyatt had remained in the saddle. Horses kept those memories. If they got a guy on the ground, they remembered. If you gave up on them, they remembered. If you stuck, they remembered.

He rode up to the gate and leaned to open it. A little more of a lesson than he'd planned, but the gelding didn't dump him. Instead he backed and then slid through the open gate with Wyatt still in the saddle.

"I'm so sorry, Wyatt." Violet smiled a little and shrugged. "I didn't even think."

He swung his leg over and slid to the ground. "Normally it wouldn't matter. He's just greener than most. The people bought him as a yearling and kept him in the field for the next two years. He hadn't been trailered or had a halter on until we brought him over here."

"And you're already riding him?"

"We've done a couple of weeks of ground work to get him to this point."

"I see." But she didn't. Violet wasn't country. She had never been on a horse. A half-dozen years ago Wyatt had still been hitting rodeos and Violet had seen it as a waste of time.

He'd quit after that year, the year he won the buckle he'd always wanted. He quit to focus on ministry, on his wife and family.

The dog ran out of the barn and barked. Another car was coming up the drive. He groaned a little. Just what he needed, Violet and Rachel here at the same time. Rachel pulled up and his girls climbed out of her car.

"She took them fishing." He explained, because Violet had been gone when he got back from church. She'd left a note that she'd be back in the afternoon and she'd spend another night before going home.

"That's good, Wyatt." Violet didn't cry, but man, her eyes were overflowing.

"They love being around her."

"Yes, they do. And she's a lovely young woman." She smiled at him as if that statement meant more. She was making a point he really didn't want pointed out.

"Violet, she isn't…"

Rachel was too close and the girls were running

toward him with a stringer of perch. He shook his head and let it go. Violet could believe what she wanted. He let his gaze slide to the woman in question, to a smile that went through him with a jolt. Her hair was pulled back in a tangled mass of brown curls and her eyes sparkled with laughter.

Violet could believe what she wanted, he repeated in his head as his attention slid back to his girls, to what really mattered.

"Did you girls have fun?" He took the string of fish and hugged the girls close. Molly and Kat wrapped their arms around him.

"We fished and waded and paddled a boat." Molly smiled a big smile. Her wounded spirit was healing. He smiled up at Rachel, knowing she was partially to thank for that. Rachel and time were healing their hearts. Kat's and Molly's, not his.

His didn't feel quite as battered, but he thanked time, not Rachel. Oh, and the faith that he'd held on to, even when he hadn't realized he was clinging to it like a life raft.

"They had lunch and on the way home took a short nap."

"Thank you." Wyatt straightened from hugging the girls, a little stiff from the wild ride he'd taken a few minutes ago. "I guess I should get inside and get cleaned up. I'm supposed to be at the church this evening to meet with your dad."

Rachel glanced at her watch. "I have a meeting, too. But first I'm going to drive up and see if Andie needs anything."

He nodded and watched her walk away. The girls were telling him all about fishing and the lake. He shifted his focus from them for just a moment to watch Rachel get in her car. She waved as she drove away, the top down on her car.

"Wendy would have liked her." Violet spoke softly and he couldn't meet her gaze. His mother-in-law liked Rachel Waters.

So where did that leave him? It left him staring after a little red convertible. The dog had come out of the barn and chased her down the drive. At least Wyatt had more sense and dignity than that.

Rachel pulled up the long drive to Andie and Ryder's house. She did a double take when she spotted a plane parked near the barn. What in the world?

She got out of her car, still looking at the plane and ignoring the border collie that ran circles around her, barking and wagging its black-and-white tail to show that the barking was meant to be friendly. She reached to pet the dog and then walked up the sidewalk to ring the doorbell.

Etta opened the door before Rachel could actually push the bell. The older woman looked beautiful as always with every hair in place and makeup perfectly applied. Today she wore jean capris and a T-shirt, no tie-dye.

"Hey, girl, what are you doing out here?" Etta motioned her inside.

"I took Molly and Kat fishing, then thought I'd stop and see if Andie needs anything."

Etta laughed. "She needs something all right. She needs off that couch. She's driving us all crazy. It's spring and she can't stand being inside."

"I hear you talking about me," Andie yelled from the living room.

Etta's brows shot up and she smiled a little, then motioned Rachel inside. She walked to the wide door that led into the living room.

Poor Andie, pregnant with twins, flat on the couch. The other option was the hospital. She waved Rachel in.

"Contrary to popular belief, I don't bite." Andie rolled on her side. "And do not call the media and tell them there is a whale beached in Dawson."

"You look beautiful."

Andie growled a little and sighed. "Right."

"It'll be worth it…"

Andie waved her hand. "I know, I know."

"And it won't take you long to get back to your old self. With babies, of course."

"It's frightening." Andie's eyes shadowed.

"Honestly, Rachel, it really is scary. Ryder and I are just learning to be responsible for ourselves, and we're going to be responsible for two little people, for making sure they grow up to be good adults. We're going to be responsible for their health, for their well-being, for their spiritual life."

"I'm sure God is going to have a little hand in it."

"Of course. And hopefully He'll get us past the mistakes we're going to make."

Rachel sat down in the chair next to the couch. "Train up a child in the way they should go."

"And when they are teens they'll rebel and give you gray hair." Andie laughed and the shadows dissolved.

"Right. I think I gave my parents more than their share of gray hair during my rebellious years."

"I can't picture it, you as a rebel."

Rachel sat back in the chair and thought about it. "I don't know if it was rebellion or just trying to find a place where I felt included."

"You?"

"Me. My sister, Cynthia, was the pretty cheerleader. Rob was studious. I was overweight and never felt like I fit in. I was always the poor pastor's daughter in secondhand clothing, lurking at the back of the room."

"I'm sorry, Rach. I wish you could have grown up here."

"Me, too. But I went through those things for a reason. I can relate to feeling left out, afraid, unsure of who I'm supposed to be. When I tell the kids at church that this stuff is temporary, they believe me."

"I love you, Rachel Waters." Andie reached for her hand. "The girls at church are lucky to have you. And before long maybe we'll also have a new youth minister?"

"Dad has interviewed a few people but he hasn't landed on the right person." Actually, her dad believed the right person was in their church and just not ready for the job. Not yet. Not until his own heart healed.

"What about Wyatt?"

"I'm not sure if he's ready."

"No, I mean, what *about* Wyatt?" Andie's smile changed and her eyes twinkled with mischief. "He's pretty hot."

"He's pretty taken and your brother-in-law."

"Taken?"

Humor and laughter faded. Andie's head tilted to the side and she waited.

"He still wears his wedding band."

"Of course. I think he hasn't thought to take it

off." Andie grimaced a little. "These two are really doing the tango in there."

"Do you need me to get Etta or Ryder?"

Andie shook her head. "Nope, not yet. It's just occasional kicks and a few twinges. When the contractions really hit, I won't be this calm."

Rachel left a few minutes later. As she drove down the drive and turned back in the direction of Dawson, her thoughts turned again to Wyatt Johnson.

He was a complication. She smiled because it was the first time she'd found the perfect label for him. Complication.

How did people deal with a complication like that, one that made them forget convictions, forget past pain, made them want to take chances?

It seemed easy enough. Stay away. That was the key to dealing with temptation, resist it. Turn away from it. Not toward it.

She'd learned to resist the lure of chocolate cake, so surely she could learn to resist Wyatt Johnson. After all, she really, really loved chocolate cake.

Chapter Ten

It felt pretty strange, walking out of church with the sun setting, and his girls not with him. Wyatt reached into his pocket for his keys. He waved goodbye to Pastor Waters and headed for his truck.

Slowly, little by little, he was getting back to his life. Or at least the life he now had. That included faith. He could deal with life, with being alive.

Pastor Waters had helped him through the anger part of his grief. Wyatt had been working through the questions that had haunted him, kept him up at night.

Why had God allowed Wendy to take those pills? Why hadn't God stopped her from getting them, or stopped her from taking them? Why hadn't God sent someone to keep her from doing that to them? To herself?

Wyatt exhaled, but it didn't hurt the way it

once did. He stopped at his truck but didn't get in. Instead he walked to the back of the truck and put the tailgate down. A few minutes alone wasn't going to hurt him. The girls were good with Violet.

He sat on the tailgate.

God hadn't stopped Wendy from breaking his heart. He closed his eyes and man, the anger still got to him. It was easier to be mad at God than to be mad at Wendy. She had made a choice. She had gone to a doctor who hadn't known about her depression, got pills Wyatt hadn't known about and had taken those pills.

After counseling. After prayer. After it seemed that she was doing better.

She'd made a choice to ignore the voice that probably tried to intervene, telling her to stop, to call someone, to give God a chance. God had been there the day she took those pills, probably pleading in His quiet way, trying to get her attention. And she'd made a choice.

Wyatt had to let go of blaming himself and God. He had to let go of blaming her. She'd been far sicker than any of them realized. She'd been hurting more than he knew.

A voice, real, clear, fresh, carried across the lawn of the church. He opened his eyes and listened to her sing. Rachel. He couldn't see her but he saw her car on the other side of the church. He hadn't realized she was still there.

He listened carefully to words that were far away. She was singing about falling down in the presence of God.

After a few minutes there was silence. The door of the church thudded closed. He watched as she walked down the sidewalk, away from him, not even realizing he was watching. He smiled a little because when no one was watching, she had a fast walk, almost a skip. She had changed from shorts and a T-shirt to a dress and cowboy boots.

A few minutes later he listened as she tried to start her car. The starter clicked but the engine didn't turn over. So much for casual spying without getting caught. He hopped down from the back of the truck and headed her way.

She sat behind the wheel of the convertible, the top down. When she spotted him she looked surprised and a little smile tilted her mouth.

"Problem?" He leaned in close and her scent wrapped around him. Oriental perfume, peppermint gum and wild cherry lip gloss.

"No, not really." She turned the key again.

"Really?"

She bit down on her bottom lip and shook her head. "The alternator has been making a funny noise. Dad said it was about to go."

"Oh. That isn't something I can fix."

"Really?" Sarcasm laced her tone and he laughed.

"Really." He opened her car door. "But I can give you a ride home."

"Thank you." She stepped out of the car. Up close the dress had tiny flowers and she was wearing a jean jacket over it. He was used to seeing her in jeans. She reached into the back of the car for her purse and the bag she carried each week. He knew it usually contained cookies and craft projects for the nursery. On Wednesdays she worked with teen girls. She was always busy.

He took the bag from her hands. "Let me carry that for you."

She smiled and let him take it. "I didn't expect you to still be here."

"I had a meeting with your dad."

"Oh, that's right."

He wondered if she knew, but he doubted she did. Pastor Waters wasn't the type to talk, not even to his family, about church business or counseling sessions.

"Have you had dinner?" He opened the passenger-side truck door for her and she climbed in.

"No."

"I would take you out, but the only thing open is the convenience store. How about a slice of pizza and a frozen slush?" He stood in the door of the truck, waiting for her answer.

She finally nodded. "Sounds good."

No, it sounded like trouble. But he'd offered and now he had to follow through. He shut her door and then he whistled low and walked around to climb in on his side.

He started his truck and backed out of the parking space. A quick glance right and Rachel was staring out the window, her hands in her lap, fingers clasped. He smiled because he hadn't expected her to be nervous.

The smile faded pretty quickly when he realized he felt a little like wringing his own hands. What was he, sixteen? Not even close. He was double that and then some. But when was the last time he'd been alone with a woman who wasn't his wife? Other than his mother-in-law or Andie, when he drove her to the doctor once a couple of months back, it had been a long time.

At least he still knew the basics. Open the door for her. Buy her a nice dinner. Or the closest thing to a nice dinner. Walk her to the door when he took her home.

Kiss her goodnight?

He shifted gears and cruised down the back road that led the few blocks to the convenience store. The evening was warm and humid. He rolled down the windows and wind whipped through the cab of the truck.

Rachel continued to stare out the window. She reached up to hold her hair in place as it blew around her face. They passed a few houses and people in their yards turned to wave. Well, at least everyone in town would know tomorrow that he'd been spotted with Rachel Waters.

Good or bad, it would get around.

"Want me to roll up the window?"

She shook her head and finally turned to look at him, smiling a little. She had a dimple in one cheek, and he noticed for the first time that her hair glinted with hints of auburn. He was a man, he wasn't supposed to remember details.

"I love this time of year."

He downshifted and turned into the parking lot of Circle A convenience store. "Yeah, me, too."

The timbre of his voice was low and husky, reminding her of fingers in her hair. Rachel swallowed at a thought that felt a little dangerous to a woman who had always been pretty happily single.

The metal building that housed the Circle A was lit up inside and out. Cars were lined up at the gas pumps and several trucks were stopped at the edge of the paved lot; teenagers hanging out on a Sunday night.

"This town never changes." Wyatt shook his head as he made the observation.

"Is that bad?"

"No, not really. I guess it's good to find a place that isn't moving too fast." He pulled the key from the ignition. "Do you want to eat at one of the booths inside?"

Orange plastic seats and bright fluorescent lights. That would just draw attention to them. "I'd rather eat out here."

"I guess we could be like the kids and sit on the tailgate."

Why that appealed to her, she didn't have a clue. But it did. She dug around in the handful of teenage memories she'd held on to and not one of them included sitting on the tailgate with a cowboy. Every woman should have that memory.

"Sounds like fun."

He shot her a look and smiled. His eyes were dark and his skin was tanned from working in the sun. He pushed the white cowboy hat back a little, giving her a better view. Who needed the Seven Wonders of the World if they could sit in a truck with Wyatt Johnson?

"So, are you coming in?"

She nodded and reached for her door handle.

This was getting ridiculous, getting lost in day-dreams that should have faded when she was sixteen, wanting things she'd thought she'd never have, with a man who clearly wasn't looking.

Butterfly, don't fail me now. She smiled a little as she closed the truck door and met him on the sidewalk. They didn't hold hands and he didn't put a guiding hand on her back. This wasn't a date, just two people having pizza.

Because her car hadn't started. She reminded herself that he was just being kind. When they circled the building and walked up to the sliding glass doors on the front of the building, their reflection greeted her. A man in jeans and a cowboy hat, a woman in a dress and boots. They looked like a nice couple, she thought.

Reminder—not a couple, just a nice guy who offered to take her home. Handsome, sweet and just a friend.

The cool air of the convenience store and the aroma of convenience foods greeted them as they walked through the doors. A few kids stood around the soda fountain, talking, laughing and being kids. Wyatt's hand touched her back and he guided her to the counter where food warmed beneath lights and pizza circled on a display wheel.

"Pepperoni or sausage?" Wyatt asked, too close to her ear. She shivered a little and shrugged. He smiled at the girl behind the counter. "Three slices of each."

She started to object but kept her mouth closed. The girl in the red apron smock opened the plastic door and slid slices of pizza into a box.

"I can get our drinks," Rachel offered. "Do you really want a slushy?"

He grinned, the way Kat grinned when she was up to something. And a slushy wasn't exactly an act of rebellion. But on him, it appeared that way. His grin was a little lopsided and his dark eyes flashed.

"I want all three flavors."

She grimaced. "For real?"

"For real."

It sounded disgusting to Rachel, but if he really wanted to do that to himself, more power to him. She held his cup under each nozzle and grabbed a bottle of water for herself. When she returned he was at the register. He eyed her water but didn't comment.

Not until they were back outside sitting on the tailgate of his truck.

"Water, seriously?"

"I like water." She took a slice of pizza from the box.

And then there was silence as they ate and watched teenagers horsing around. One girl tried too hard. Rachel sighed because she remembered trying too hard. She remembered chasing the boys, grabbing them, laughing too loud.

"Another slice?" He held out the box but she shook her head.

"Two is enough for me."

He set the box down next to him and nodded at the teenagers. "That really takes me back."

"Yeah, me, too." Rachel leaned against the side of the truck bed. "But I bet we have different memories. You were that boy, the one with the swagger and the grin."

A boy in jeans, a T-shirt and boots, with the big truck and the bigger smile.

He grinned and tipped his hat back. "Yeah, I guess I was."

"I was that girl." She pointed to the girl who was grabbing the boys and staggering just a little. Rachel wanted to rescue her, to pull her out of the crowd and tell her to love herself.

Closing her eyes, it was too easy to be that girl, to feel so insecure, to want so much to be loved and not getting that it really did have to start with accepting herself. She really hadn't gotten it, that she couldn't force people to love her.

"You okay?" The words were soft and a hand touched hers.

Rachel opened her eyes and smiled. "Just remembering."

"What's wrong with that girl?" Wyatt didn't look at the girl. He watched her instead. She shrugged and avoided what she knew would be a questioning look, but she felt his gaze on her, felt his intensity. "She looks like she's having fun."

"She isn't having fun. She's trying to find someone who will love her."

He didn't respond. She turned to look at him, smiling because she hadn't meant to delve that deeply into the past.

"That was you?"

"That was me."

"I can't imagine."

"I've gone through some changes since then." Another reason for the butterfly, a reminder that life has a way of changing things. Every season brings something new.

She hopped down from the back of the truck. "We should go."

He nodded, agreeing. Instead of commenting, he grabbed their trash and carried it to the barrel at the corner of the store. Rachel opened her door to get into the truck, but she shot one last look back at the kids. They had a beach ball, bouncing it in the air from person to person. Another truck pulled in. More kids got out. The young girl she had watched raced around the crowd, frantically trying to be a part of something.

A deep ache attached itself to Rachel's heart, remembering that person she'd left behind. But when Wyatt got behind the wheel, she questioned if she really had, or was that insecure girl still hiding inside her, wanting the love that Rachel insisted she really didn't need.

The lights of the parsonage glowed a soft yellow from behind gauzy curtains. A motion light in the backyard came on as Wyatt pulled the truck to a stop. He shifted into neutral and set the emergency brake. Rachel was already reaching for the door handle.

He should let it end that way, with her getting out, him letting her walk up to the door. But a butterfly tattoo and the hurt look that had flicked across her features as they'd sat eating their pizza kept him from listening to common sense.

Later he would regret this moment, he knew he would. He would regret not listening to the part of him that wanted to remain detached. Instead he got out of the truck and met her as her feet hit the ground.

"I can help you get your car to the garage tomorrow."

"Dad can take care of it." Her eyes were huge in the dusky night.

Another moment that he'd have to think about later: looking a little too long into those eyes. But looking into her eyes didn't begin to compare to the need to hold her. His hands were shoved into his pockets and he fought the part of himself that didn't want to get back in that truck and drive away.

She sighed and her lips parted, not an invitation, he didn't think. No, she was probably going to say something. She probably should tell him to back off or hit the road. Either of the two would work.

A thinking man would have given her a chance to say one of those two things. An idiot cowboy like him didn't always think things through. Sometimes guys like him just had no sense at all and they acted.

That's what he did, he acted, freeing his hands from his pockets and tangling them into masses of brown curls that smelled like wild flowers. He breathed deep as he leaned toward her. He hovered for a second, giving her one last chance to send him packing. When she didn't, he touched his lips to hers.

For a long second she didn't react, but then she moved and her hands touched his arms. He drank her in, steadying himself with one hand on the truck door behind her. Man, she was sweet. The kiss was sweet. Her hands moved to his back, holding him close. That was sweet.

He pulled back, resting his forehead against hers because he couldn't really breathe. Or think.

And then reality came rushing back in, hitting him full force with a load of guilt and remorse. Those shouldn't be the emotions a man felt after a kiss. She deserved more than a guy tied to the past.

"I'm sorry." He whispered close to her ear, wanting to pull her back into his arms. Instead of giving in, this time he stepped back.

"Yeah, I knew you would be." Pain flickered across her features, hard to miss, even in the dark.

"What do you mean?" He jerked off his hat and swiped a pretty shaky hand through his hair.

Her expressions changed to compassion. She reached for his hand. "I just kissed a married man."

He pulled his hand loose from hers, too aware of the wedding ring he'd never taken off, and aware of the message it sent. He shoved his hat back on his head and took a few smart steps back.

It hurt to breathe and hurt worse to think about her words. She hadn't moved away from his truck until that moment and as she stepped past him, she paused to touch his cheek, her smile was soft and sweet.

"I know you loved her. You really don't have to explain or apologize."

"Yeah, I do." He said the words too late. She was halfway to the house and he was standing there like a fool. Her dog ran out of the house, past her to him. The big shepherd circled him a few times, growling. Her whistle called the animal off.

The drive home didn't take near long enough. He had two minutes to get it together. He felt like he needed two hours. Or two days. A man didn't kiss a woman like that and just walk off.

Rachel was the kind of woman looking for forever, not stolen moments at the end of the night. And Wyatt didn't know if he'd ever want to do forever again. But he did have to think about the future and about the ring still on his finger.

As he parked, lights flashed off in the upstairs room that belonged to his girls. He sat in his truck and watched as other lights came on. Violet waiting for him to come home.

He needed to get his act together. He leaned back in the seat and stared at the barn, at the glimmer of moon peeking through the clouds. At stars glittering in the clear patches of sky.

For eighteen months he'd been asking himself the question he had wanted to ask Wendy. Why had she left them? He let out a tight sigh that came from so deep inside him that it ached. Had she stopped loving them? Had she been unable to love them? He rubbed a hand across his face, clearing his vision.

It was wrong to blame her. He'd even come to terms with the fact that he couldn't blame himself. Now he had to come to terms with the fact that she wasn't coming back. Guilt, accusations, anger— none of that would bring her back.

He put his hands on the steering wheel and the gold band on his left hand glinted. He raised his hand and shook his head. Maybe it was time to let her go, to move on with his life.

Or maybe it wasn't. He'd deal with one thing at a time.

It took a minute to get the ring off, twisting and sliding it over his knuckles. His finger felt bare. His heart felt even worse. He slipped the ring into his pocket and opened the door of the truck.

Violet walked out the back door. He walked across the yard, his vision blurred. He took in a deep breath and let it go.

When he walked up the steps of the porch, Violet gave him space. She followed him inside and instead of asking questions she started a pot of coffee. Good thinking, because it looked like it might be a long night.

When she turned, her eyes were misty and her smile trembled on her lips. "Are you okay?"

"I am. Thank you for staying with the girls while I helped Rachel out."

"Where else would I be? Wyatt, you didn't stop being my family when…" She bit down on her bottom lip and blinked a few times. "You're my kid. Those are my sweet granddaughters up there. You're all I have left of Wendy, and I don't ever want that to end. No matter what happens in the future, I hope to always be your mom."

He hugged her and she eventually pulled away and reached for a tissue, pulling it from the box on the counter. She wiped her eyes and smiled.

"Violet, I thank God every single day for you and you'll always be in our lives."

"That's good to know because I can really be a pain sometimes and I need people who will put up with me."

He laughed, and pulled two cups from the cabinet over the coffeepot. Violet sighed a little and he turned.

"You took off your ring."

He looked at his left hand and nodded. "Yeah, I did."

Because of Rachel Waters. He didn't have to explain that to Violet. He guessed she probably knew. She probably understood better than anyone else in his life. Maybe even better than he understood it himself.

Chapter Eleven

The dog slid through the door ahead of Rachel. She kicked off her shoes and pushed them up against the wall. She dropped her purse next to them. She hadn't come in right away. After that moment in the yard with Wyatt, she had needed a few minutes to clear her mind and get it together before she faced her parents.

As if she was still fifteen and trying to hide something.

She was twenty-nine and really not a child.

In reality she was a long, long way from childhood and innocence. She sat down at the kitchen table and moved a few pieces of the puzzle that had been there for days, unfinished. The painted faces of kittens on cardboard were scattered, unrecognizable. She found an edge and slid it into place.

Her life was just as scattered, just as in pieces as that puzzle. She had kissed Wyatt Johnson. Her parents had decided to take the church in Tulsa and she couldn't tell anyone until the formal announcement. She had to bury the pain of moving and leaving this place behind.

She had to leave Wyatt and the girls. She hadn't expected that to be the part that hurt the most. She hadn't expected to feel anything for Wyatt other than sympathy.

Surprise. The feelings were unexpected after years of holding back and waiting for God to bring someone into her life. She moved another puzzle piece and a ring on her own finger glinted in the soft light of the kitchen. A purity ring that she'd put on after some very bad relationship choices.

She had made a promise to wait for God to bring someone into her life. She had made a promise to herself to stop pursuing and to wait for someone who loved her enough to pursue her. She figured the fact that she was nearly thirty said it all.

"Hey, kiddo, how's your car?" Her dad stood in the doorway, the tie from earlier in the day gone, but he still looked like Pastor Waters. She smiled and pushed the other chair out with her foot, an invitation.

"It'll have to go to the garage. The alternator finally gave up and died."

"I'll have it towed to Grove tomorrow."

"Thanks, Dad."

"What's up?"

"Nothing."

Robert Waters crossed the room and sat down across from her. She smiled up at him because this was a scene that had played out a lot in their lives, the two of them together with a puzzle between them. He started moving pieces and she did the same.

"This move isn't what you want, is it?" He looked up, smiling a little. "You don't have to go."

"I know that. I want to go."

He pushed a piece of the puzzle into place and they finally had an entire kitten. She was allergic, so this was the closest she got to fuzzy felines.

"Rachel, promise me you'll tell us the truth. If you don't want to leave, you shouldn't. You know that Etta would gladly let you stay with her."

"I know that, but Etta isn't my family."

"No, she isn't." He piled up gray puzzle pieces that went to the gray kitten she was working on. Rachel reached and took one that might fit.

"Dad, I'm okay with this." She smiled because she was okay. It wasn't her first move and she knew that moves were never easy. But she was okay. She would adjust.

She was used to leaving places, leaving people. Doing the right thing didn't always mean the right thing felt good. Sometimes doing the right thing was difficult.

Her dad stood up. Before he walked away, he leaned to kiss the top of her head. "Your mom said to tell you goodnight and she loves you."

"Right back at her." She reached for his hand to stop him from walking away. "Don't worry about me."

"I always do. That's part of being a parent. We want our children to be happy."

She nodded but this time she didn't answer. She didn't know how to respond to being happy. Her heart had gone into rebellion and suddenly wanted something she knew she couldn't have.

The best way to get her heart into check was to explain to it that she had just experienced something that everyone experiences: a goodnight kiss. It had been nothing more and nothing less, just a kiss at the end of a sweet evening with a man who might possibly be a friend.

To make it anything more than that was a mistake. Like telling him he was still wearing his wedding ring. She cringed a little because it wasn't her place to point that out to him, not a man who had been kindness itself. He had kissed her goodnight. It wasn't as if he'd proposed.

Wyatt Johnson was sweet and gorgeous. He wasn't looking for long-term.

She moved another piece of puzzle into place and got up to go to bed. Tomorrow she'd apologize.

The crazy gelding jumped sideways and lurched. Wyatt held tight, wrapping his legs around the animal's belly. If he'd been paying attention instead of thinking about holding Rachel last night, maybe he wouldn't have been in this position. The horse beneath him shook his head and hunched again. Wyatt held tight, waiting. The horse settled into a jarring trot across the arena.

He'd be glad to send this one back to his owner. If it wasn't for the fact that he liked to tell people he'd never met a horse he couldn't break, he'd probably send the horse back today.

He glanced to the side, making sure the girls were still on the swing. They were. As he watched, Molly jumped up and started waving. He caught a glimpse of an old truck. Molly waved and ran.

The horse unleashed on him, bucking across the arena. Hooves beat into the hard-packed dirt of the arena. Wyatt pushed his hat down and held tight, his teeth gritted against the jolt that set him a little back in the saddle. The horse lurched again, this time nearly getting him off the side.

He barely made it back into the saddle when the crazy animal's head went down and his back end went up. Wyatt felt himself leave the seat and go airborne over the horse's head. He heard Molly scream and then he hit the ground.

Pain shot through his back and head. He rolled over on his back and worked to take a deep breath. He bent his knees and blinked a few times to clear his brain.

This couldn't be happening.

Rachel yelled his name. Good way to be calm, Rachel. He shook his head. The girls were screaming. He rolled to his belly and made it to his knees. Oh, yeah, he'd been here before, sucking in a breath that hurt like crazy.

"I guess this is a bad time to tell you I saw a few of your cows out on the road?"

The voice came from his left. He rolled his head that way and tried to smile. But smiling hurt, too. He was way too old for getting thrown.

"Yeah, this might be a bad time."

"Want help?" Rachel reached for his arm. He gritted his teeth and pushed himself to his feet with her hand holding him steady.

"Daddy?" Molly's voice trembled. He blinked and focused on her face, just behind Rachel.

"I'm okay, sugar bug." He drew in a deep breath. "Wow."

"Should I call…" Rachel bit down on her bottom lip and shrugged a little.

An ambulance. Good not to say it around the

girls and panic them more than they were. He shook his head and regretted it because it felt like it unhinged his brain a little.

"You can call Greg Buckley and tell him to come and get that crazy horse of his. I'm done with that animal." He'd been fighting that crazy buckskin every time he got in the saddle.

"You think?" She smiled and his girls followed her example. "What about those cows?"

"Daddy, are you broke?" Molly stared up at him, eyes full of unshed tears.

"Nah, of course not."

Violet headed their way, picking through the dirt and rocks with high heels that he would have laughed about if he'd been able to laugh. "Do you want me to drive you to the hospital?"

She'd been packing her stuff, getting ready to go home. Now he had other concerns.

The girls. He sucked in a breath that hurt like crazy. And crazy wasn't the word he really wanted to say. A lot of other words came to mind. He leaned on the fence, draping his arms over the top rail. The girls.

He shifted to look at Rachel.

"Could you stay with the girls?"

"Of course I can. Or I can drive you."

"No, Violet can take me." What he didn't need or want to do was lean on Rachel. Literally. He didn't want to be in pain in front of her. It didn't do a guy's ego any good to have to lean on a woman to make it to the car.

"Daddy?" Molly stared up at him, brown eyes wide.

"I'm fine, Mol. You stay with Rachel and I'll be home later."

"Do you need help?" Rachel had stayed next to him, smelling soft and sweet. And she was asking if he needed help.

Even if it killed him, he wasn't going to lean on anyone.

"I'm fine." He touched Molly's cheek and she smiled. "Be good."

She nodded and grabbed Kat's hand. "We will."

He never had a doubt. But would she be afraid?

"Okay, let's go." One last deep breath, and then he headed for Violet's car with steady steps that said he would be fine.

Violet walked next to him. "You're such a tough guy."

"Yeah, well, we wouldn't want the girls to see me cry." He gritted the words out from clenched teeth.

"Are you really going to cry?" Violet teased as she opened the passenger-side door.

He waved at Rachel and the girls. "Not on your life, Violet."

"You cowboys think you're so tough."

Yeah, that's exactly what he thought.

Violet slid behind the wheel of the Cadillac and turned the key. As she shifted into reverse, she glanced his way. "How badly are you hurt? No lies this time."

"I haven't lied yet." He leaned back into the soft leather seat. He wished his truck felt this good. "Maybe ribs, maybe my back."

"How are you going to take care of the girls when I leave? You've vetoed every applicant I've interviewed. What do we do now?"

"I can take care of my girls, Violet."

"I know you can, but this changes things."

"You have me in the ICU and I haven't even made it to the E.R."

"I'm thinking of all the possibilities."

"Well, I'm not. I'm fine and I'll be home by dinner. I have a birthday party to plan. Molly will be four next week."

"I know. I had planned on going home to get a few things done and coming back before then."

"And you can still do that." He closed his eyes and counted to twenty.

As he counted he heard her phone dialing. He opened his eyes and waited.

"Rachel, this is Violet. Oh, no, honey, we haven't made it to Grove. No, but I need a favor. I'm taking

John Wayne to the E.R., but he's probably going to need help when I leave. I haven't hired anyone because he's picky. I know you have a lot going on, but if you could take the job temporarily." Short pause and he wanted to jerk the phone out of Violet's hand. "Just for a month or until we can find someone."

"Violet." He whispered what she should have seen as a warning. She smiled at him and kept talking.

"That's great, honey. I'll write you a check when we get back. Or when I get back. Right, just keep the house clean, cook some meals and make sure the girls have clothes that match."

"I can dress my kids." He pushed the button to recline the bucket seat. "Women."

Because of a woman he'd taken his ring off last night. It was all connected: the kiss, her words and removing his wedding ring. He just didn't want to draw the lines, not at the moment.

Maybe it was just about letting Wendy go. Maybe it was about Rachel. Right now he needed a shot of something and a lot less thinking going on in his scrambled brain.

Chapter Twelve

"What do we do with that horse?" Rachel looked down at the girls. The two of them shrugged. Of course they didn't know. They were two and four. Or almost four.

Molly was about to have a birthday. Rachel worried her bottom lip thinking about that special occasion and the possibility that Wyatt would stay in the hospital. Okay, horse first, cows in the road second. Or maybe the cows should be first.

She pulled the phone from her pocket and called Ryder.

"Ryder." He answered with his name and he sounded stressed and frazzled.

"Ryder, it's Rachel. Listen, Wyatt got thrown and Violet is taking him to the E.R."

"Oh, that's just what I need."

Okay, not the response she expected. "Ryder, you guys have cows out, just a few hundred feet down from your drive. And I have this horse here, the one that dumped him, and…"

"Rachel, I'm sorry, I can't. Andie's having contractions. I'm flying her to Tulsa."

In the background she heard Andie yell that she wasn't getting in a plane with him. Rachel smiled and waited for the two to argue it out and remember that she was on the phone.

"Rachel, I'll call Jason and see if he can put those cows in. Can you handle the horse?"

"I don't know. I can try."

She looked at the horse in the arena. The buckskin stood at the far corner. He needed the saddle and bridle removed and he needed to be put in the field. Or maybe a stall. She wondered which one.

"If you can't get him, call Jason or Adam."

"Okay. Is there anything I can do for you and Andie?"

"Pray."

The conversation ended and she was on her own. Rachel looked at Molly and Kat. No help there. They both looked pretty nervous. Molly's dark eyes overflowed with tears.

"I want my daddy."

"I know, honey." Rachel squatted in front of the girls. "I know you're worried about your daddy.

He's fine. Remember when he left, he was talking. He even walked to the car. He's fine."

"He'll come home." Molly sobbed and rubbed her eyes.

"Of course he will." This wasn't normal fear. Rachel hugged the girls close. "He'll be fine. And while he's gone, we'll be fine. We'll get that silly horse taken care of and if we need to, we'll put the cows in. We can do that, can't we?"

Keep them busy. That's all she knew to do.

But it meant walking into the arena with a horse she didn't trust. She straightened, trying to look taller, and gave the horse a look. As if that would do any good. A hand tugged on hers.

"You aren't gonna ride him." Molly wide-eyed and maybe a little impressed.

"No, honey, I'm not. I'm going to unsaddle him and—" she bit down on her bottom lip "—I'm going to put him in a stall."

Molly grabbed her hand and with her other hand she grabbed hold of Kat. "We'll go with you."

"I appreciate that, Molly, but I think I should go in alone."

It sounded like a movie, as if they were going into a house with monsters, or some horrible villain. It was a horse, a tan horse with a black mane and tail. Just a small little horse. Well, maybe not so small.

"You girls wait out here." She handed Molly her phone. She didn't say to call 9-1-1 if something happened. Instead she smiled as if she was brave and not shaking in her shoes.

She whistled, kind of. The horse shot her a disinterested look. Okay, she was used to that look. He must be a man. She smiled at her joke and kept walking. The horse didn't move.

"Buddy, it would help me out if you'd play nice."

The horse reached his nose under the bottom rail of the fence and nibbled at a few blades of grass. Rachel walked up to him, talking softly, saying a few prayers under her breath. Did horses smell fear? She really hoped not.

She reached for the reins that had been dragging on the ground. The horse snorted and raised his head. He jerked away from her but she held tight.

"Listen, horse, I'm not a cowgirl like Jenna and Andie, but I do know how to hold on tight. I am not going to let you win."

The buckskin edged close and snorted, blowing grass and grain all over the front of her shirt. "Oh, that's real nice."

She held both reins and led the horse back to the barn. He plodded along behind her as if he was Kat's little pony. She rubbed his neck as they walked.

"So now you're going to be nice?"

For a brief moment she relaxed but then she remembered how it felt when she watched Wyatt go flying from the horse's back. She didn't want to remember how it felt to watch him hit the ground and stay there, motionless.

From across the arena she heard her phone ring. She glanced back. Molly held it up.

"Go ahead and answer it. Tell them I'll call back." She didn't want to yell, to startle the horse.

She had decided the best course of action was to unsaddle him, take off his bridle and leave him in the arena. She could get him a bucket of water and hay.

First, the saddle. She wrapped the reins in a hook on the wall of the barn and the horse stood perfectly still. She pulled the girth strap loose and eased off the saddle. He moved away from her and she thought about how easy it would be for him to turn and kick.

Instead of thinking about that, about possibilities, she unbuckled the strap on the bridle and pulled it over his ears and off his head. The horse stood for a moment, a little unsure. Finally he backed away from her and turned to trot to the other side of the arena.

She had done it. Now to take care of the girls. She turned as a truck pulled up the drive. Jason Bradshaw. He hopped out of the truck and headed her way, his big smile making things feel better.

"You got him unsaddled." Jason opened the gate for her. "I'll put him in a stall and feed him for you."

"What about the cows in the road?"

Jason picked up Kat and tickled her until she laughed. "I put them back in and fixed a loose section of fence. Have you heard anything yet?"

"Not yet. I don't think they've had time." She glanced at the girls because she didn't want to have this conversation in front of them.

Jason sat Kat on the back of Rachel's truck. He motioned for her to walk with him. Rachel followed. The cowboy, his red hair cut short, had a smile that made everyone feel better.

"Rachel, do you know about the girls?"

"I'm not sure what you mean."

Jason rubbed his jaw. He glanced from her to her truck where the girls were waiting. "This should be up to Wyatt, but there's something you should know. In case Wyatt doesn't get home tonight, you need to understand that Molly gets pretty upset when he isn't here."

"I'm not sure if you should tell me something that Wyatt hasn't told me."

"He'd want you to know. For the sake of his girls. Molly and Kat were with Wendy. They were alone until he got home that afternoon and found them."

And she got it in a way that ached so deep inside her she didn't know if she could draw in a breath. She thought about those two little girls alone with their mother. But Wendy wouldn't have been with them. She took the pills and left them alone.

Rachel turned away from Jason because it was too much to know this secret about the wife that Wyatt had loved. Still loved.

But he'd taken off his wedding ring. She'd noticed it as she'd helped him up. She wondered if it had been about the kiss or what she'd said. Or had it been something he'd been working up to and he finally realized it was time?

"I should take them inside and fix their dinner."

Jason walked with her back to the truck. "He doesn't tell people because it's Wendy's memory. He doesn't want that to be what people think about when they remember her."

"I understand."

Jason lifted Molly and Kat out of the back of the truck. He gave them each a hug as he set them on the ground. "You girls help Miss Rachel.

She's going to stay with you until your daddy gets home."

"Will he come home tonight?" Molly held on to his hand.

"I'm not sure, Molly. He might come home tonight. Or maybe tomorrow. Either way, he'll be fine and so will you. Rachel is going to stay with you."

She was staying. She smiled at the girls. They looked at her, both wide-eyed and full of trust. Of course she was staying.

It was after midnight when Wyatt walked through the front door of his house. He had eased up the front steps because two steps were easier than five or six when a guy had a few cracked ribs and a couple of pulled muscles. Oh, yeah, and a concussion.

He didn't remember, but the horse must have landed a good kick in his side as he went down.

Violet walked behind him. Poor Violet, he guessed she really wanted to go home after a week of the drama in Dawson. He smiled because she hadn't said too much. She'd actually been pretty terrific, fighting with the doctor when they wanted to keep him overnight.

No way could he leave his girls overnight. He knew the look of terror in Molly's eyes when she thought he wasn't coming home. He remembered eighteen months ago walking through the front door and finding her in the playpen with Kat. The two had been red-faced, eyes swollen from crying and nearly breathless from sobbing. That memory would never leave him.

"Wyatt, you have to let your mind rest." Violet touched his arm. "I know that look on your face. I know what you're thinking. The girls are fine. I've never seen them better."

"I know." He took careful steps into the living room. He'd sleep on the couch tonight instead of climbing the stairs.

But the living room was occupied. He stopped in the doorway. Molly and Kat slept on the couch. Rachel slept curled up in the chair near the couch. A fire, only embers, glowed in the fireplace. It felt good and smelled good. The temperature outside had dropped after a late-evening storm rolled through. The fire was pretty inviting.

Yeah, right, the fire.

"This is sweet." Violet touched his shoulder. "Now where are you going to crash?"

"The sofa in my office." He didn't move, though. Either because it hurt too bad or, he looked at the girls and at Rachel Waters, it hurt too bad. He smiled at Violet. "What about you?"

"I'll stay up with you."

"You should get some sleep." He nodded toward the stairs. "Go, Violet, I'll be fine."

"I'll stay up with him." A sleepy voice from the living room interrupted their conversation. Rachel stretched and sat up. "I've been sleeping for a few hours. You go to bed, Violet."

He really didn't need a babysitter. He considered arguing, but he didn't have the strength and he knew he'd never win against two women. Rachel was already on her feet, a blanket around her shoulders.

Blame it on painkillers or a concussion, but he wanted to say things he wouldn't be able to take back in the morning.

"He has to be woken up every hour." Violet explained what the doctor had told them. He kept his mouth shut, glad she'd stepped in and kept him from making a complete fool of himself.

"I can do that." Rachel stood, folding the blanket that she'd had over her.

"I really don't need a keeper. This isn't my first concussion or the first time I've cracked a few ribs." What he didn't want to admit was that it hadn't hurt as bad as this the last time.

"Right." Rachel smiled at Violet who said good-night and then retreated up the stairs. He watched her go and then he was alone with temptation itself. She smiled at him, completely unaware of how beautiful she was standing in that spot with just a sliver of moonlight coming through the window and the warm embers from the fire reflecting the auburn highlights in her hair.

Yeah, guys weren't always clueless.

"I'm not sure if this is right or wrong." He eased a step in her direction and braced a hand against the doorway.

"What?"

"This." He reached for her hand and pulled her close. She stood in front of him, unmoving, unblinking, staring at him as if he'd lost his mind. Maybe he had. Maybe the horse had knocked him silly. Maybe it had knocked sense into him. Whatever it was, he didn't want to think too deeply, not yet.

"This." He whispered it again and leaned, touching his lips to hers. She was so sweet, like cherry soda on a hot summer day. She was his first time driving alone, the first horse he owned, the first time he'd ever felt free. She was everything and more.

She healed his heart with that kiss. She made him feel things he hadn't expected, had never felt.

And she scared the daylights out of him. He moved his hand from her arm to her back and he held her close, trying to breathe, trying to get it right and trying to convince himself to let her go.

Eventually she stepped back. Her lips parted and she shook her head. "No."

"No." Did he want to argue with her or agree? He wasn't sure.

"This isn't what you want." She smiled a little. "This is about feeling vulnerable and alone. This isn't about us. This is something you have to work through, on your own."

He looked a little deeper and saw her pain. It shimmered in her eyes and he remembered the other night on the tailgate of his truck when she'd talked about girls trying too hard to be loved.

Her story. Man, he wanted her stories.

"You should lie down." She swallowed and looked away.

"I should." He laughed and it hurt like crazy. "I think I might need help."

"The sofa in the office."

"Yeah." Cowboy up, Wyatt, he told himself. A guy couldn't impress a woman if he had to lean on her just to make it to a chair. Casual would work. He draped his arm around her shoulders.

"That's a lame move." She left it there, though.

"It's all I could think of right now." He walked next to her, pretty thankful for a strong woman who felt soft and smelled sweet.

"Stop sniffing my hair." She whispered the warning as they walked through the office door.

"Sorry."

She laughed and shook her head. "My dog has more manners."

"Not possible."

"I'm sure of it." She stopped in front of the couch and slid out from under his arm.

With her hands holding his arms, she held tight while he lowered onto the couch, trying hard not to groan. He gritted his teeth instead. She smiled, not the kind of smile that meant sympathy.

He really wanted sympathy. A nice pillow, a soft blanket and maybe a glass of water. She didn't look as if she planned to play nursemaid. More than anything she looked like someone about to escape.

He was the guy who needed to let her go because that made sense. Getting tangled up in this didn't. He'd seen tangled up before. He'd doctored a horse for a week because it hadn't had the sense to stay out of barbed wire.

Yeah, he had more sense than that horse.

Chapter Thirteen

He looked pitiful, miserable actually. His dark hair was a mess, hanging across his forehead. The top two buttons of his shirt were gone and he still wore the jeans he'd been wearing when he hit the ground. Rachel stood for a moment, unsure of what to do next. Her internal alarm sounded, telling her to find the nearest exit and leave him to his own devices. But she had promised to stay with him, and Violet looked worn out. The girls were sleeping in the living room.

"You should take your boots off and I'll find a pillow and blanket." Good first step.

He grinned and shook his head, "Honey, I'd love to take off my boots, but I don't think I can lean down."

Okay, she didn't need this. Instead of discussing, she knelt and reached for the heel of one boot.

She slid it off and reached for the other. "Your feet stink."

He laughed a little, but she heard the grimace of pain. "Yeah, I bet they do. Thank you for taking one for the team."

She looked up, mid-pull. He was watching her. She looked away quickly and finished the second boot. As she stood up, he wrapped his legs around hers, right at her knees, and held her in front of him.

His smiled changed from soft to rotten, lifting at one corner. No, no, no. Rachel didn't want this thin strand of emotion connecting them. She didn't want to get tied into this when he was having fun, or using her to get past something.

She'd been used before and it wasn't going to happen again.

"I'm going to get you a pillow." She stepped out of the circle of his legs and moved to the door. "Ice water?"

He nodded and she left the room, walking down the darkened hallway to the kitchen. Her heart hammered in her chest and she worked to get a deep breath.

"Okay, God, give me strength." She pulled a glass out of the cabinet and instead of heading for the fridge, she looked out the window, watching trees blown by a south wind and paper fluttering end over end across the lawn. Another storm was blowing up. Clouds were eating up the dark sky, blotting the moon and the twinkling stars.

Give her strength. More than that, help her find peace. Help her to not rush into a relationship with someone who was emotionally tied up and working past his grief.

She filled the glass with ice and water. Now to find a pillow and blanket. She had seen them the day she cleaned, in a closet off the main bathroom. She flipped on the light, dug around in the closet and headed back down the hall.

He was sleeping when she returned to the office. Stretched out on the couch, one foot on the floor and his arm flopped over his face. It would be good if he stayed asleep. She put the glass down and unfolded the blanket.

"I'm not cold." He moved his arm and there was no smile. His chest expanded with a heavy sigh. "I'm scared to death."

"Why?"

She couldn't have this conversation standing. She pulled a chair close to the couch and sat down. He reached for her hand, holding it, looking at it, running his fingers over hers. He had rough, warm hands. The hands of a cowboy, a rancher.

"Wyatt, it's just a concussion. Right?"

He smiled up at her, still holding her hand. "I'm

not afraid of that. I'm afraid of you. I'm scared to death to feel what I feel. I'm not ready."

Slam. She drew in a shaky breath and pulled her hand from his. Be afraid of death, she wanted to tell him. Be afraid of the dark. Be afraid of anything, but not her.

But wasn't she scared to death of him, of being used, of being rejected?

She looked up, gathering strength and trying to find God. All of those words and then to hear that he wasn't ready. She reached for the pillow.

"You'll want this." She waited for him to lean forward and she slid it under his head. "And now, I should go."

"But…"

"I'm not leaving. I'm going in with the girls. These are not the words I want to hear in the middle of the night." She felt wrung out, exhausted, run over. "I'll be back in an hour. If you need me, I'm across the hall."

"Rachel?"

She shook her head as she walked out the door and back to the living room where the girls were sleeping. She couldn't respond, instead she brushed away tears and buried her face in the pillow she'd been using earlier in the evening.

Nothing had ever hurt this bad. He wasn't ready. She wondered if he would ever really be ready.

The awkward teenager she had been taunted her, telling her she'd never be the person he moved on with.

Tonight she fought back. God hadn't made her an awkward teenager. She was more than that. She knew that He didn't create mistakes. Every inch of her was designed by God.

The young girl who had wanted nothing more than to stay in one house was designed by Him. The teenager who had turned to chocolate and cheesecake, later to a reckless crowd of friends, and the twenty-year-old who had finally gotten it right, they were all the same person, His creation, fearfully and wonderfully made. It had just taken her a while to figure it out and to stop fighting who she was. It had taken her a while to trust Him with her life.

It had taken her a while to be comfortable in her own skin and to love herself enough to stop punishing herself.

Tonight the girl who wanted to be loved was fighting tooth and nail, wanting to believe a cowboy like Wyatt Johnson could really, really love her someday.

And maybe her parents' plan to move had come at just the right time. Maybe this move was designed to protect her heart.

* * *

Wyatt cracked one eye and saw two little girls leaning close, whispering for him to wake up. After a long night of hourly wake-up calls, this time waking up felt great, even if he didn't know how to take a deep breath and his head ached as if he'd been hit with a sledgehammer. At that moment it was all about Molly and Kat leaning over him, studying his face with worried little expressions.

"Daddy, are you awake?" Molly leaned, her nose close to his. "Because we didn't know if you would wake up."

He wrapped them both in one arm and pulled them to him. "I'm definitely awake. And I love you both."

"Grandma left." Kat kissed his cheek. "And said you had to be good and listen to us and to Rachel."

"Rachel?"

Molly nodded, all serious and wide-eyed. "Rachel told Grandma she'd be our nanny and clean our house. And she already cooks good."

"Really?" He smiled, even though it hurt.

"She doesn't need books to make pancakes. They aren't even frozen first."

"Really?" He growled and pretended to get her arms. "Can she do that?"

Molly shook her head. "She doesn't have whiskers, Daddy."

Now that was something he did know. "You're right about that. Now help me up and we'll go see about that bad ol' buckskin."

"Rachel unsaddled him."

"That's good." They each had hold of a hand and he groaned as they pulled him to a sitting position. "Man, I'm sore."

"Grandma said you've been run over by a truck, but it was just a horse."

"She meant I feel like I've been run over by a truck."

Kat held on to his hand. "Mean old horse."

"Yeah."

They led him down the hall. The aroma of bacon lingered in the air. He hoped there was some left for him. On top of that, the house smelled clean. He glanced at the clock. It was just after nine in the morning. A clean house and breakfast. Not too shabby.

Rachel walked out of the laundry room carrying a mop bucket. Her hair was braided and she had changed into shorts and a T-shirt. He knew now that she jogged nearly every day. He'd seen her a few times in the last couple of weeks.

"Seems like I might be Rip Van Winkle. Everything changed while I was sleeping." Including her, his feelings and his house.

He ambled into the kitchen, working on casual when he felt as cagey as a penned-up cur dog. He poured himself a cup of coffee and took a piece of bacon from the plate near the stove. When he turned around she was in the kitchen, taking up space, moving around as if she belonged there.

It shouldn't bother him, that Violet had hired her, but it did. He wanted to choose the person who came into his home. He wanted to choose someone who didn't smell so stinking good and who didn't look prettier than a rodeo queen, even in those faded shorts and a T-shirt.

"I'll make you pancakes." She had the fridge door open, blocking her from his view. Molly, not even four, was sitting on a stool smiling at him as if she knew way more than he was saying.

He shot his daughter a look and she giggled. The fridge door closed and Rachel's eyes narrowed as she stared at him. It took him a second but he worked up to innocent and shrugged, as if he didn't know what his kid was all about.

"Sit down and I'll fix your breakfast."

He pulled out a stool next to Kat. Okay, maybe this wasn't so bad. What could possibly be bad about sitting here watching her in his kitchen?

"I should feed the animals before I eat breakfast."

She turned, a spatula in her hand. "I took care of it."

"You fed?" He didn't feel like smiling now.

"No, I called Ryder. Of course he's in Tulsa with Andie, but he sent Jason over to take care of things. And Jackson Cooper…"

He raised a hand to stop her. She flipped the pancakes and he had to wait a second for her to get back to him. This was getting a little crazy. He was feeling pretty crazy on the inside.

Emotions should be gradual, not wildfire, spreading every which way. But he didn't think emotions came in gradual increments. Pain—Bang. Grief—Bang. Anger—Bang. Now this—Bang. He didn't want to put a name on it.

Oh, wait, maybe jealousy. He lifted his coffee cup and took a few drinks. She flipped pancakes onto a plate and set it in front of him with butter and syrup.

"Jackson doesn't need to come over here. I can manage things myself." He jabbed a knife into the butter and spread it over the tops of the pancakes.

"Right."

"Yeah, right. Cracked ribs and a concussion, that's it, Rachel. I really don't need all this help."

He wasn't some namby-pamby sissy. He'd been bucked off more bulls than he could count. He'd been thrown by horses. He'd been run over and stepped on.

"Fine, you can call Jackson and tell him you can do it yourself."

Okay, that made him sound like a three-year-old tackling a flight of stairs by himself. He chewed on pancakes that were so good he forgot to be mad.

Instead of anger, he felt a big urge to hug her. Molly giggled again. He looked down and she laughed harder.

"What's so funny?"

She giggled more. "You're funny, Daddy. You're not mad, you're happy."

Well, that just about beat all.

He kissed her cheek. "You're right, Molly Doodle, I'm happy."

As he finished the plate of pancakes, he watched Rachel move around his kitchen. He was happy. Bang. Just like that.

Being happy should have been something he grabbed hold of and thanked the good Lord above for. Instead he questioned it, a lot like the Israelites had questioned everything God did for them in the wilderness.

And on top of that, he felt guilty. The bad thing about guilt is that it undid happy.

He finished the pancakes and got up to carry the plate to the sink. Rachel took it from his hands with a smile.

"I can get it."

She rinsed it off and put it in the dishwasher. "So can I."

"Fine. I'm going to go outside and check on that buckskin. Did Jason call to see if they would pick him up?"

"I think they're getting him this evening."

He nodded and then he backtracked to the fact that she'd mentioned Ryder and he hadn't really paid attention. He blamed it on the concussion.

"What was that about Ryder?"

"Andie was having contractions. Ryder flew her to Tulsa yesterday. They called earlier and she's resting. The contractions slowed down, but they think it will be in the next day or two."

"Ryder, a dad. That's going to be fun to watch."

"He's ready for it. He has you."

Now what did he say? He stood there, aching from the inside out thanks to cracked ribs and some deep bruises. He tried for casual and leaned hip against counter, arms crossed in front of him. Rachel's narrowed gaze went from his chest to his face. She cocked her head to the side.

"I'm going outside." He eased across the kitchen.

"Don't do too much too soon," she warned softly.

"I'm not. I can't stay in the house."

"I know." She picked up the bottle of pills he'd left on the counter and tossed it. He caught it.

"I don't need these. I don't want to feel sleepy all day."

"If you're sleeping you won't be doing something you shouldn't do."

He laughed because what he was thinking and what she was thinking were two different things. Maybe she had a point. Maybe drugging him was the best thing for both of them.

"Rachel, I'll take a few aspirins, not these. And I am going outside to check on things."

She shrugged and walked away. "Suit yourself."

Right, he would suit himself. Kat and Molly were sitting on their stools watching him and watching Rachel. He brushed a hand through his hair and smiled at his girls.

He'd pick getting thrown from a horse every single day of the week over the mess Violet had made of his life by hiring Rachel Waters.

Rachel started her car and leaned back in the seat, catching her breath while the top went back on the convertible. She reached for her sunglasses to fight the sun. She was going home for a few hours and later she'd return to Wyatt's to fix dinner for him and the girls.

One last glance back at the house and she pulled onto the road and headed home. She had chores to do there, too. She had her sheep. Her mom would need help with laundry. There was plenty to keep her busy.

Including packing. As she pulled into the garage she thought about that, about packing things up again. This time she really didn't want to go. And what would she tell Wyatt? What would she say to the girls, to Molly and Kat?

Complicated. Life was very complicated. She closed her eyes and thought about that, and she tried to grab hold of God's perspective. To Him it wasn't all that complicated. She had to trust His plan.

He hadn't opened all of these doors and brought her here for no reason. Maybe He had planned for them to be here just to help Wyatt and the girls through this difficult time. And when she left, there would be someone else to help.

Maybe Wyatt would find his way back to faith and take a job in the church.

The door to the house opened and her mom smiled.

"How was the first day?"

Rachel rolled her eyes heavenward. "Not easy. A sick man is a difficult man."

"That's how they are. And he just called."

"Called here? Is he okay?"

"I think your cell phone battery must be dead. He said it went right to voice mail."

"Oh, it might be." She pulled it from her pocket. Sure enough, dead. "What did he want?"

"Andie's having the babies. He wondered if you would ride with them to Tulsa. He didn't say it, but I wonder if he isn't supposed to drive?"

"Probably not, but he isn't going to give up that information." She didn't want to go. Her emotions were wrung out and what she really wanted was to stay home and be safe. Home with her parents, no pressure, no difficult thoughts to sort out.

"Do you want your dad to drive them?"

"No, I can do it. It's just that I know we need to start packing. I planned on helping you for a few hours."

Rachel's mom stopped her, putting a hand on her arm. "Rachel, I can pack. Your dad has already started. We've done this so many times, I think we know how to get it done."

"But you need my help."

"Tonight Wyatt and the girls need you."

More people needing her. She didn't really know

if that's what she wanted for her life. And when she left, what then?

Not that he couldn't replace her with someone just as capable, maybe more so. There were plenty of people looking for jobs and several in the area who would be great with the girls.

"I'll call him and see what's going on. But I need to change clothes and get cleaned up." She'd been cleaning and cooking all day. No one would want to sit in a truck with her for an hour.

Cooped up in a truck. With Wyatt.

Not exactly the thought she needed while trying to convince herself that she needed to do this. Of course she wanted to, though. Andie might be having the babies. That was something Rachel didn't want to miss out on.

Thirty minutes later she parked next to Wyatt's garage, under the carport. He walked out of the barn as she got out of the car and reached in for her overnight bag. She watched him walk toward her, limping a little, a tiny bit stiff. He pushed his hat back and smiled.

"Nice to see you again."

"Yes, again. Do I need to get the girls ready to go?"

"I think probably. Molly is upstairs packing a bag. She's going to be four this weekend, so she's positive she can do it. I'm sure she'd let you help out, though." He pulled off his hat, smiling. "She said I can't help."

She knew he wasn't a lot of help in the clothing department, but he probably didn't need to hear that from her. But the birthday, that definitely needed to be discussed.

"Her birthday. Have you ordered a cake?"

"No, I planned to do it tomorrow." He rubbed his cheek and half smiled. "I'm not good at birthdays. Worse at buying their clothes. I really stink at the girl stuff."

Slow, steady breath. "I can help. I can even bake the cake, if you'd like."

"I'm keeping you from your life. What about Etta? I know you've had things to do that haven't gotten done because of us."

"Etta is having a slow period. She calls when she needs help."

"So this isn't taking you away from something else?"

"Not really." Just packing and telling this life goodbye. That happened to be something else she wasn't ready to tell him. Her dad would share the news with the congregation Sunday. She planned on telling Wyatt before then. She didn't want him to hear it from the pulpit, from her dad.

"Rachel, if you have other things to do, I really can do this alone."

She smiled. "I don't mind. And while we're in Tulsa we can shop for birthday presents and summer clothes for the girls."

"Now that's a good idea. You probably know how to match things."

"Maybe a little better than you."

He leaned against her car, smiling.

"I should go inside."

He edged away from the car that she thought had probably been holding him up. "We'll leave as soon as I get finished feeding. Adam is going to feed tomorrow."

"I'll make sure things are closed up inside the house."

He flashed her another smile. "Thanks."

Leaving had never been easy. This time it would feel like tearing her heart out. She watched him walk away, a little slower but still with that confident cowboy swagger.

He would never know what these weeks meant to her or how much it hurt to go. What difference would it make if he did?

She only had to remind herself what he'd said last night. How could she forget? He'd kissed her silly and then said he wasn't ready.

Chapter Fourteen

Wyatt stared through the window into the NICU at the two little girls, Ryder and Andie's babies. They were close to five pounds each, but Amelia needed oxygen and they were watching Annette. Two more A names. He shook his head, a little in awe over the whole situation.

His little brother was a daddy.

Molly and Kat stood on a stool and watched their little cousins. He couldn't help but think about their births. Molly's had been a happy occasion. But Kat's birth… He wrapped an arm around a little girl who had never really had her mother. Wendy had tried. He knew she'd tried. What a rough few years.

And lately? Things were changing. The weight on them wasn't as heavy. The girls smiled more.

The common denominator happened to be in the other room with Andie, hugging her, praying with her. He'd said his own prayers on the drive here, that the babies would be safe and healthy.

He tugged down on his hat, because he wasn't about to cry. But man, his eyes burned. Little babies did that to a guy. A hand slapped his back. He grimaced, cringing a little.

"Oh, sorry about that." Ryder grinned and pointed to his little girls. "Aren't they something?"

"Yeah, hard to believe you could make something that pretty."

"Don't make me have to take you outside and whoop you, not today." Ryder draped an arm over Wyatt's shoulder. "They look like Andie. Ain't that something?"

"Yeah, funny how that works." He glanced down at his own girls and saw their mother in them. He still had her, in them, in their smiles, their eyes. In Kat's spunky nature. In Molly's laugh.

"We're going to have to get busy and have some boys to protect these girls." Ryder smiled into the NICU window. "Yep, I'm starting to see why the Coopers had all them kids."

"I guess having the boys is up to you."

"Ah, come on, you could have a little boy in the next year or two."

Wyatt shook his head and gave his brother a look. "Ryder, I don't even know where you're going with this conversation. But let's just stick with the idea that you're married and before you know it, you'll have a son. Poor kid."

"I think Andie isn't going to want to have another one for a while." Ryder's smile softened. Andie had done that, turning him from a boy to a man. "Wendy's gone, Wyatt."

"I think I know that." He looked around. The girls had wandered back to the sitting area and weren't paying attention to their uncle Ryder.

"I know you do. No one knows it better than you. But seriously, Wyatt, it's okay to find someone else."

"Right."

Heels on the tile floor. He turned and smiled at the woman walking toward him. Her hair hung in loose curls that framed her face. She smiled a little, her eyes misty and her lips trembling. She bit down on her bottom lip and blinked a few times.

Babies did that to people. Not to him, of course. He turned back to the window, the babies that were wiggling and scrunching up those wrinkled little faces. He'd always said babies weren't really as pretty as people said. He was rethinking that.

"Aren't they beautiful?" Rachel peeked over his shoulder, her chin touching, resting on him.

"Yeah, they sure are." He caught her reflection

in the mirror. She backed away but she still stared at those babies. Twin girls with downy soft, blond hair.

"You guys staying the night in Tulsa?" Ryder glanced from Wyatt to Rachel, smiling. Wyatt shot him down with a look.

"Yeah, we've got a couple of hotel rooms. Molly already informed me she's staying in the room with Rachel."

Kat was hugging Rachel's leg. He figured he'd lost her, too. And it was okay. He was fine with that. He was kind of losing himself, too.

"We're going shopping tomorrow," Molly piped up, smiling big with tired eyes. Wyatt picked her up and she wrapped her arms around his neck. Man, this was what life was all about.

"I'm going to have that." Ryder had the look of a man who had just gotten it.

"Yeah, this is it, Ryder. Good times and bad, it's all about this." Wyatt hugged his daughter and rubbed his cheek against hers. "This is what makes it all worth it."

"I have to go see Andie." Ryder blinked a few times.

Wyatt slapped him on the back and then he turned to Rachel. Ryder was already down the hall, turning the corner. Wyatt slipped an arm around Rachel's waist and, as if she knew, she took Molly.

He took a good deep breath and kept his arm around the woman at his side. Sometimes it just felt good to have someone to lean on. He remembered last night, holding her, teasing her.

"What now?" He didn't really know what he meant by that. "Something to eat? Shopping?"

Rachel held Molly and Kat walked next to her. Both girls were dragging. "Both, if they don't fall asleep in the car."

"Right." He held his arms out to Kat. "Come on, Kat, I can carry my girl."

She grabbed his hands and he picked her up. Rachel smiled but she didn't say anything. Yeah, fine, it wasn't as easy as it should have been. But Kat's arms clung to him and she buried her face in his shoulder.

Yeah, it was all worth it.

After shopping with two toddlers, Rachel's feet hurt and she was ready for a cup of coffee on the balcony of her room. She kissed Molly and tucked the blanket in close. The child wrapped sweet arms around Rachel's neck and smiled.

"I love you, Molly."

"I love you."

Rachel's heart melted. She leaned to kiss the

little forehead again. Kat, next to Molly in the queen-size bed, slept soundly. She'd fallen asleep as soon as they got her into her jammies and tucked her in.

"Go to sleep." She tucked Molly's blankets again. "I'll be sitting on the balcony and I'll leave the door open a crack."

"You won't leave?"

"I won't leave. Promise. I'll be on the balcony and I'll be here with you in the morning."

Molly nodded and smiled.

One last kiss on the cheek and Rachel walked away. She poured herself a cup of coffee and stirred creamer and sugar in it. When she turned, Molly's eyes were closed. Sleeping already. Rachel smiled and walked quietly past the bed toward the glass doors that led to the balcony.

A movement on the balcony caught her attention. Wyatt. They had separate rooms but shared a balcony. He stood at the wrought iron railing, leaning against the support post that ran from the floor to the upstairs balcony. When she opened the door, he turned.

"It's a nice night," he commented as he turned back to the view of the skyline.

She nodded, but he probably wasn't paying any attention. It had been that kind of day, the kind that wrung a person out and left them empty. The babies, the memories and she was positive he was in more pain than he let on. It hadn't been an easy day.

"Coffee?"

He shook his head. "No, thanks, too late at night."

She sat down and held the cup in her hands. Tulsa evenings were beautiful. It was a little warm, a little humid and traffic honked on the city streets. She put her feet up on the chair next to the one she sat in.

Wyatt left the rail and sat next to her. He moved slower but broken ribs didn't seem to be something that slowed him down. He told her it wasn't the first time he'd cracked a few ribs and probably wouldn't be the last.

She sipped her coffee and he rubbed his shoulder and neck. Try as she might, she couldn't ignore him, couldn't avoid watching him. His profile was dark, his expression impassive. Rachel sighed and set her cup down on the table. She moved her chair closer to his, her heart catching a little.

No going back.

But did she really want to move forward? She closed her eyes and waited for common sense to return, to drag her back to sanity. She had made so many reckless decisions when it came to relationships. Worse, she had tried to make people love her.

Her hand was on his shoulder, the knotted muscles were tense beneath her touch. She opened her eyes and he turned, his expression questioning. The words from the other night came back, that he wasn't ready.

After a long moment he reached for her hand and pulled it forward. With her pulse fluttering at the base of her throat, he brushed the back of her hand with a sweet kiss. "Good night, Rachel."

"Good night?"

"Yeah, time for you to go." He smiled at her. "I think we both need space and maybe fresh air. Alone."

She couldn't move.

"Rachel, this is me being a gentleman and not a rogue cowboy. This is me making the right choice for both of us. I'm not sure what to feel right now and I don't want to hurt you."

"Not sure?"

He shrugged. "Until recently I still felt married to a woman who isn't coming back. I still have a lot to work through and I don't want to hurt you."

"I'm not going to get hurt. I'm a big girl."

He smiled at that. Her hand was still in his. He squeezed her fingers lightly and let go.

"I know you are, but I'm not willing to be the one who hurts you."

Rachel picked up her cup but she didn't move from her seat. He was telling her to go, but the look in her eyes said something else. She knew, of course, to back off, to not take things where they shouldn't go. She moved her chair away from his, giving them both space.

"Wyatt, what was she like?"

He stared off into the night and didn't answer right away.

"I'm sorry, I shouldn't have asked."

"No, it's okay, I'm just surprised." Wyatt sighed. "I can talk about her. For a long time I couldn't, but now, it's been eighteen months and I can talk. I can tell you that she loved our girls. Man, when we had Molly, Wendy glowed. She loved that baby."

"I'm sure she did."

"She loved her, but…" He stared out at the night, away from her. "She left us. She held Molly, she fed her and sometimes she laughed. When we had Kat, Wendy disappeared inside a shell. She stopped taking care of herself. She didn't take care of the girls. I took her to doctors, to counseling…"

"I'm so sorry."

He nodded. "Yeah, me, too. I had some pretty wonderful years with a woman that I thought I'd spend my life with."

"I think she probably wanted the same thing." Rachel didn't know what else to say. She had seen his pain, but hearing it made it all the more real.

It put everything into perspective.

She stood and he looked up, smiling. Her hand trembled as she reached to touch his cheek. His eyes closed and he leaned into her touch. Her heart couldn't decide if it should fast-forward or pause.

"Good night, Wyatt."

As she walked through the door she heard him sigh and she echoed the gesture. Walking away was something every girl, every woman should know how to do.

And sometimes, she knew from experience, it wasn't easy. Sometimes there was a cowboy on the other end of the emotional tightrope.

She closed the door and bolted it. She pulled the curtain closed and locked the connecting door between their rooms.

The phone rang. She picked it up, glancing quick at the girls. Kat slept on, Molly's eyes fluttered a little.

"Hello?"

"It's me." His voice was soft, not sweet, not this time.

"I kind of knew that."

He laughed. "Yeah, well, I wanted to apologize. I just wanted to say that I'm trying not to lead you on."

"I'm not going to let you." She sat on the edge of the desk and held the phone with her shoulder. "Wyatt, I'm…"

"Rachel?"

"I was a really wild teenager and I made a lot of mistakes, mistakes I regret and that I've worked to get past. I'm almost thirty years old. I know what I want. I know what I'm waiting for. I'm not chasing you."

She closed her eyes and told herself how stupid that sounded. She'd spent the last few years thinking that God would send someone if there was someone for her. And now she was telling this man she wasn't going to chase him. Stupid, stupid, stupid.

"Rachel?"

"Yeah?"

"I think you're amazing." She could hear his smile.

Amazing. Right. He didn't know that she was trembling from her head to her toes. Fear?

"Thanks. Good night, Wyatt."

She put the phone in the cradle, her hand on it, waiting. It didn't ring again.

* * *

Wyatt pulled up the drive to his house. The girls were sleeping in the backseat of the truck. Rachel hadn't said much on the drive home. He hadn't pushed her. After last night it seemed like a good idea to keep quiet.

Breakfast had been a quiet affair on the balcony of their hotel. The girls had eaten cereal from room service, Rachel had eaten fruit and yogurt. He'd felt pretty guilty eating biscuits and gravy. They'd had lunch at the hospital cafeteria.

The twins were doing great. Amelia was breathing on her own now. Wyatt breathed a sigh of relief over that situation. At least that, if only that, was going right. He, on the other hand, had a big mess to clean up. He had a woman sitting next to him and he didn't have a clue what to say to her or how to fix things.

How did a man move on when, until eighteen months ago, he'd planned on spending his life with one woman, raising their children, growing old, serving God? And then it had all changed. Yeah, move on. That's what people were telling him. Time to move on, Wyatt.

He stopped the truck and just sat there. Rachel opened her door but she didn't get out. He shot her a look and she didn't smile. Of course she didn't.

He hadn't given her a lot to smile about. He really wanted her to smile.

He really wanted to explain to her how it felt to try this moving on stuff. It hurt like crazy, deep-down hurt. It hurt the way it had when people had tried to tell Wendy to just get over it, take a shower, go for a walk. And she hadn't been able to do those things.

He sat there for a second, thinking. Maybe it didn't hurt as much as he'd thought it should? The thought hit like a ton of bricks, the knowledge that getting over his pain could hurt, too. He sure hadn't planned on that.

"I'll carry the girls in for you." She stepped out of the truck and looked back in at him.

Oh, no way was she doing this.

"I can take the girls in, Rachel." He got out and opened the back door to reach for Molly. She woke up enough to crawl into his arms. "Come on, kiddo, you can take a nap inside."

"I want a pink cake for my birthday," she whispered close to his ear.

"A strawberry cake?" He held her close, his ribs hurting like crazy.

"No, just pink. A pink cake." He carried her up the back steps. Rachel followed with Kat.

"Well, then, we'll find you a pink cake."

"I can make her a cake." Rachel had opened the other door and reached in for Kat. "If you want."

"I think she'd like that. We usually buy one from the store."

Last year they hadn't had much of a party. It had been the three of them and a store-bought cake. Her third birthday and he'd put candles on her cake and later, after the girls had gone to bed, he'd stood outside and bawled like a baby. He'd had a fight with God, then he'd shifted his anger to Wendy.

The dog ran around the side of the house, wagging his tail, glad to see his people home. Wyatt carried Molly up the back steps and into the house. Rachel was behind him with Kat. He opened the door and nodded for her to enter first.

"Do you want me to fix something for dinner?" Rachel asked as she carried Kat through the house to the living room.

"No, I'll take the girls to the Mad Cow. Why don't you go on home? I'm sure you have a life that doesn't include us."

She shifted her arms and placed his daughter on one end of the sofa. When she turned, her smile was vague. He placed Molly on the other end of the sofa. Her eyes opened and she smiled.

"I'm not tired, Daddy."

"You don't have to sleep, honey." He turned and Rachel had found an afghan and was covering

Kat with it. "Seriously, though, if you have things to do…"

"I actually do. My mom needs help with some things."

"They're lucky to have you."

"I'm lucky to have them. They've always been there for me. Now it's my turn to be there for them."

She picked up her purse and he walked out with her. They'd left her car in the carport, but it was still covered with green pollen. He waited while she dug through her purse for her keys. When she found them, he opened the car door for her.

"Rachel, if you need a couple of days off to get other things done, I understand."

"I might. There's something…" She sighed. "Never mind. I'll see you tomorrow."

"Are you sure?"

She got in the car and he rested his arm on the vinyl top and looked in.

"I'm sure. I'll see you tomorrow. We have a lot to do before Molly's birthday Saturday."

"Okay, I'll talk to you later." He closed the door and backed away from her car. As she backed out of the carport, he waved and she smiled.

It seemed normal enough, but it didn't sit right. Whatever she had started to tell him mattered and he wanted to know what it was.

Chapter Fifteen

Boxes lined the walls of the living room and Rachel didn't want to empty the contents of the room into the brown cardboard. She sat down on the footstool and stared at the bookcases, the curio cabinet and the pictures on the walls. She loved this room with its pine-paneled walls. She loved the hardwood floors and the big windows.

She loved this house.

"The boxes won't pack themselves."

She turned and smiled at her mother. It was a good week. Maybe the excitement of the move had given Gloria Waters the extra energy. Or maybe her immune system was in check. Either way she had accomplished a lot in the two days since Rachel had been gone.

Twenty-nine years old, Rachel shouldn't be having this conversation, about moving, about starting over with her parents. She pulled a few books off the shelves and held them. Her mom walked into the room and sat in the rocking chair across from her.

"Rachel, don't go. Stay here."

"That's out of the question." Rachel stacked the books in the bottom of a box. "I'm not going to stay here when the two of you are going to Tulsa."

"Are you afraid?"

Afraid? Rachel looked out the window. Across the road the neighbors were mulching their garden. Down the street a new neighbor had moved in. Her dad had already invited them to church. A church that would soon lose its pastor. She thought about that church, her teen girls, her Sunday school class and the nursery.

Rachel always became involved in her dad's ministry. The new church was larger, had quite a few paid staff, he'd told her. She didn't know what that meant for her. But the real reason she would go would be to help her parents. She cooked when her mother didn't feel up to it. She kept the house clean.

Afraid?

"Afraid to jump out there, find someone and fall in love. Are you afraid? I know that Tanner hurt you, but it was a long time ago."

Rachel didn't know how to process what her mother had just said. Tanner. She hadn't really thought about him in years. They had dated when she was twenty.

"It isn't about Tanner." About a man who had dated her for a year and then decided he couldn't handle her faith.

"I wonder sometimes. I know he hurt you."

Rachel smiled at that. "It hasn't hurt in a long time, Mom. I'm here because I want to be here, to help you and Dad. And I guess because I haven't found anyone to spend my life with."

"You will, honey."

"Will I?" She shrugged. "I don't know if I will. If I don't, it's okay."

"What about Wyatt Johnson?" Her mom smiled that secretive smile.

"Mom, I'm not fifteen and I haven't been doodling his name in my notebook. I love his girls and I'm glad I could help out, but that's as far as it goes."

Heat worked its way up her cheeks and she reached for another stack of books. Now if only her mom would walk away and let it alone. Instead, Gloria Waters laughed a little.

"I think it's far more than caring about his girls."

Rachel grabbed more books and stacked them in the box.

"Mom, Wyatt Johnson is a nice guy who still loves the wife he lost."

"He might always love her, Rachel. That doesn't mean he can't love someone else."

Rachel finished packing the shelf and her mom continued to rock in the rocking chair. When the bookcase was empty, Rachel turned to face her mother.

"Mom, he might love someone else someday. I'm not going to push myself into that position. It doesn't work that way."

She knew from experience.

"Does he know that we're moving?"

"No, I haven't told him. I started to, but I know that Dad is going to make an announcement this Sunday and I didn't want it to get out before Dad could tell people."

"Well, I think you ought to tell Wyatt. He's going to need someone to take your place, or a chance to talk you into staying. The more time you give him, the better."

Someone to take her place. The words ached in her heart. That meant someone else taking care of Molly and Kat, someone else coloring with them and helping them draw pictures of flowers and kittens. She had only been in their lives since last fall when Wyatt came back to town. The idea of leaving them shouldn't create an empty space in her heart.

But it did. All of the years of holding back and not getting attached and two little girls had changed everything. Two little girls and their dad, his smile, his eyes, his sweetness. She looked up, caught her mom watching her.

"You shouldn't let this go, honey."

"You're not giving up, are you?" Rachel smiled and folded down the flaps of the box.

"Not on your life."

At least someone had hope for her love life. Rachel had given up a long time ago. True, Wyatt made her want to have hope again, but common sense told her to go slow and not act impulsively.

What if she put her heart on the line, even stayed in Dawson, only to find out that he would never be ready to move on? Or when he was ready, what if it was with someone else?

Either could happen. Rachel smiled at her mom.

"I'm fine."

Her mom touched her shoulder and left the room.

Rachel opened another box and went for the curio cabinet. She packed porcelain dolls, a tiny vase and her heart. All the breakables went together in a box labeled "Fragile."

* * *

The horse lunged in a slow circle at the end of the rope Wyatt held. The doctor had told him to stay off horses for a couple of weeks. That was fine and dandy, but he couldn't stop working. A few years ago he would have ignored the doctor and went ahead with whatever he needed to do.

Now he had the girls to think about. He glanced behind him. They were on the swing, not going very high but jabbering nonstop. He started to turn back to the horse but caught a flash of red on the road. Rachel.

She'd taken yesterday off. The girls had missed her, moping around the house because he had fed them some kind of casserole he thought would be an easy fix. He'd been pretty wrong about that. His cooking skills, with or without Etta's cookbooks, were not improving.

The red car eased up his driveway. He hadn't expected her today either. There were a lot of things he hadn't expected but he didn't want to dwell on them. The girls jumped off the swings and started across the yard. He would have yelled for them to stop, but they paused a good distance from the driveway and the car that was pulling up.

He gave a quiet command and the horse stopped, waiting for him to walk up to it. He left the rope on the ground and the horse remained steady in the spot where he'd come to a halt. Ears forward, the animal turned its head toward him.

"Good job, boy. Real good." He unsnapped the lunge line and replaced it with a lead rope. "Let's get you out to pasture and see what's going on."

He led the horse to the gate and turned him loose. The animal went off at a fast trot, shaking his head. After a few minutes he burst into a full run, bucking his back end into the air. Wyatt turned and walked back toward the house and the girls. And Rachel.

"What are you doing here?" He opened the gate that led to the yard.

"Thought I'd stop and check on the girls and find out if you've heard anything about the twins."

"The twins will probably be home by the first of next week." He picked up Kat, wincing a little at the catch in his ribs. "Sis, you're getting heavy."

Kat shook her head no and rested her chin on his shoulder.

Rachel smiled at the girls and not at him.

"So, what's really up?" He put Kat on the ground. "You girls run and play."

Kat and Molly started to protest, but he shook his head. They ran for the swings, forgetting to be upset. He smiled as he watched Molly help Kat onto the lower swing.

Rachel stopped walking. She watched the girls, her eyes a little misty. "I came over to bake the cake for Molly's party tomorrow. But before the party and before church Sunday, I want you to know something. I want you to hear it from me."

"Okay." He pulled off his hat and waited.

"My dad is taking a church in Tulsa. My mom needs to be closer to the doctors there. They want to be closer because they're getting older and they feel like it will be better for them."

"I hate for the church to lose your dad." He waited, wanting to hear that she wouldn't leave. He glanced in the direction of the girls, wanting it to be about them. "Rachel, the girls love having you here."

"I know. I love them."

Unsettled shifted to anger. "You're trying to tell me that you're going, too, right?"

"I am." She continued to watch the girls play, but her eyes filled with tears. He watched one slide down her cheek and then the next.

"I'd like for you to stay. We could work something out if you wanted to work for me full-time."

"I can't." She wiped the tears away, one finger across her cheek. "My brother and sister live so far away. I'm the only one here to help my parents."

"I see." He rubbed the back of his neck and

couldn't think of a thing to say that didn't sound crazy.

He didn't want to hire another housekeeper. Joint cream and therapeutic socks were no longer appealing. He kind of liked butterflies, country music and the smell of wildflowers.

The thoughts were pretty dangerous and he didn't want to go there. He'd taken his ring off. Now he was contemplating how to keep Rachel Waters in his life. No, in his girls' lives.

That's why he needed Rachel. She made Kat and Molly smile again. She made them happy. And that made his life a lot easier.

"Would you think about it? Just consider it. If you don't want to leave, the job is yours."

"Thank you. And I will think about it." She smiled and the gesture trembled on wild cherry lips. He was about as confused as a man could get.

"Well, I guess you have to make this decision. I need to feed the girls lunch."

"I can help."

He brushed his hand through his hair and settled his hat back on his head. "If you have things to do, I can handle it."

"I came over because you need help. I'm going to fix lunch and then I'll get something in the oven for dinner."

"Right, that works." He leaned against her car and he couldn't look at her. "Man, this is rough."

"I'll be around for the next month. I can even help you find someone."

"No, I don't want to do this again." He managed a smile. "Maybe you can teach me to cook before you leave."

"I can do that. And for the next couple of days, we have a lot to do to get ready for Molly's party."

"Yeah, her birthday. She's counting on you for that. I can't braid hair and I sure can't decorate for a little girl's birthday."

"I'm not going to miss her birthday, Wyatt. I'll go ahead and bake the cake today. I'll decorate the cake and the house tomorrow before her guests arrive."

"Thanks, that'll be great."

She nodded, her smile still soft and trembling. "I'm sorry. I love the girls. I don't want them to be hurt."

"Yeah, but they will be. I know you have to go. I get that. But the girls are my priority."

"That's the way it should be."

"Well, I have to get back to work."

"I'll take the girls inside to help me with the cake."

He nodded and walked away.

This wasn't the way he'd expected his day to go. He'd almost prefer to get kicked by a horse. At least with a horse he knew what to expect.

Some things in life were honest and easy, always what you thought they'd be. And sometimes one choice changed everything. Jackson Cooper's words wormed their way into his mind. Rachel had definitely gotten under his skin.

But worse, she'd made Kat and Molly pretty happy. For the first time in a long time they'd felt whole, the way a family should feel. Because of her.

And now they were back to square one.

The cake baked in the oven, making the kitchen smell like strawberry. Rachel had explained to Molly that pink cakes sometimes had flavors and since they were using a mix, pink happened to be strawberry. The little girl had stopped being offended after a small taste of batter confirmed that pink was not only a pretty color, it tasted good, too.

"What now?" Rachel leaned on the counter across from the two girls who sat on stools sharing a plate of cookies.

"We should draw pictures," Molly informed her, dipping a cookie in her cup of milk.

"Or play with frogs." Kat nodded her head, milk

dripping down her chin and a circle of chocolate around her mouth.

The back door slammed shut. Rachel straightened and waited for Wyatt to join them. She heard him in the laundry room and then he was there, tall and lean, his jeans faded. He must have hung his hat in the laundry room because the crown of his hair was flattened from having worn it all day.

"How about the Mad Cow, girls?" His smile didn't include her. Rachel didn't blame him.

"Rachel is making omelets." Molly picked up her cup to drink her milk. "Because eggs are good and we have stuff to do."

"What stuff?" This time he did look her way, his brow arched in question.

"Party stuff. We're going to decorate for tomorrow." Molly clasped her hands together and leaned toward her daddy. No way would he deny that little smile.

"I tell you what, you girls decorate. I'll order from the Mad Cow and bring it home for us." He shifted to face her. "If you write down what the three of you want and call in the order, I'll run upstairs for a quick shower and a change of clothes."

In a month, life would be ordinary again, missing them, missing Dawson. Rachel smiled because it didn't do her or the girls any good to let those thoughts take over.

He smiled back and then he left. She watched him leave, wondering how much pain he was in. He hid it well, his pain. The girls were tugging on her, asking questions about the cake and ice cream that she promised to make. Homemade, with strawberries, of course.

The oven timer went off. She grabbed an oven mitt and pulled out the cake. Strawberry pink. She put it on the top of the stove. The aroma filled the air, even stronger than when it had been baking. Both girls were off their stools and standing a short distance away.

Rachel wanted cake. She wanted chocolate. She really wanted to not be this new person she'd created, the one who jogged instead of eating cheesecake when she was depressed.

"It's going to be good." Molly grinned big.

"It is going to be good. And we'll put pink icing on it and pretty stuff."

"Flowers? And a ballerina?"

Rachel smiled. "Yes, flowers and ballerinas. We bought those in Tulsa, remember?"

"Bought what?"

Wyatt stood in the doorway dressed in khaki shorts and a T-shirt. His feet were bare and his hair still damp from the shower. His tanned skin looked darker thanks to the white T-shirt.

"Decorations for the cake." Rachel ached inside because something had happened, something was gone and she knew she'd miss it for a long, long time after she left Dawson.

The thin thread of connection they'd shared had been broken. Because she was leaving and he didn't want his girls hurt. She didn't want them hurt either.

She was torn. Did anyone get that? She felt so responsible for her parents. She loved this town. She smiled at Kat and Molly. She loved them.

"Did you make the list of what we want to eat?"

She picked up a pen and grabbed a tablet from the basket on the counter. "Okay, what does everyone want?"

She didn't look at him and she hoped he wasn't looking at her. Kat jumped up and down and said, "I want fries."

"More than that, Kat." Wyatt smiled at his daughter.

Rachel wrote down the rest of the order. "I'll call Vera."

"Okay, let me know how long it'll be. I promised the girls they could ride their pony for a few minutes."

Both girls shouted and started to jump around the room. Wyatt smiled, watching them. And Rachel watched him. Molly and Kat ran into the laundry room to pull on boots and hats. And suddenly Rachel didn't know what to do, didn't know where she fit.

She knew she never wanted to leave here. The thought settled deep, like most bad thoughts. How many times had she moved as a kid? She'd lost track.

But she wasn't sixteen looking for a place to start over. She was nearly thirty and some unseen clock was ticking an unfamiliar beat, one she hadn't expected.

Once again her gaze traveled to that cowboy. It was his fault, that much was obvious. It felt pretty good to blame him for making this difficult.

Kat and Molly returned wearing their boots and with cowboy hats on their heads. She smiled at little faces that were starting to tan. They had matching braids that stuck out from beneath their hats. Cowgirl hats, Molly had informed her, were important for cowgirls. They had bought one for Rachel, too.

She didn't look as cute in a cowgirl hat as they did.

She wouldn't need one in Tulsa. She turned away from the happy scene and started dishwater for the few mixing bowls and spoons she'd used to make the cake.

Footsteps behind her. She felt him close, felt the warmth of his exhaled breath, inhaled the spicy cologne he wore. His hand touched her arm.

"You okay?" His voice was close to her ear and she nodded, looking out the window at the barn, at fields with grazing livestock, at the dog sleeping under the shade of an oak tree.

"Yeah, I'm good."

"No, you're not."

She shook her head. She wasn't at all good. She was breaking inside, not just her heart but all of her. Because she loved them. She loved the girls and she loved him and for a few brief weeks she'd been a part of their lives, a part of their family. She didn't want to leave them, or Dawson.

She closed her eyes and waited for an answer, even a whisper. Nothing. Of course nothing, God knew. He had known this plan and He knew the rest of the untold story. He knew how much it hurt.

"I'm going to take the girls outside." His hand dropped from her arm. "You were good for us."

She closed her eyes and listened to him walking away from her. She wanted him to beg her to stay. Of course he wouldn't do that. He wanted her help finding a replacement because she really was just the housekeeper and the nanny. She wasn't a part of his family.

She wasn't… She opened her eyes and watched him with the girls, watched him hug them, watched him pick Kat up and set her on his shoulders, grimacing just a little as she settled.

She wasn't the woman he loved. How could she stay here working for him, feeling the way she felt? How could she stay here when she knew that her parents needed her?

In the end it was easier to walk outside and pretend she wasn't leaving. It was easier to watch the girls laugh as Wyatt led them on the pony and pretend she would always be in their lives.

Chapter Sixteen

The birthday party had been a pretty big success thanks to Prince the pony. Wyatt sat back in the lawn chair and watched some of the last visitors leave. He smiled at the sight of the poor pony with pink and purple ribbons in his mane and tail. That had been Rachel's idea. It had seemed pretty goofy to him, to do that to the poor pony. The kids had felt differently about it. Little girls loved ribbons. He'd have to remember that.

Little girls loved pink cakes and balloons. They loved pretty dresses and dolls, even when they were cowgirls with ponies and stock dogs. Rachel had taught him that about his daughters. She had taught him a few things about himself, too.

Someone sat down next to him. He turned and smiled at Robert Waters, Rachel's father. The older man smiled back and stretched long legs in front of him. He wore his customary slacks and button-up shirt.

Wyatt glanced down at his own khaki shorts and leather flip-flops. He smiled at Rachel's dad.

"Glad you were here." Not so glad to hear that you're leaving. Since that wasn't common knowledge, Wyatt didn't mention it.

"Wyatt, Rachel told me that she shared with you that we're leaving. The elders know and a few others. I'll make the announcement tomorrow."

"I'm sorry to hear that you're going." Wyatt let out a sigh and shook his head. "The church hoped you'd stay a long time."

"You know as well as I do that we can never make plans for God." Robert crossed his left leg over his right knee, still relaxed, always relaxed. He was about the calmest man Wyatt had ever met.

"Yeah, things do happen without our permission."

"Have you given any more thought to the youth ministry? When I asked you to do that, I didn't know we were going to be leaving. I guess God did."

"I've thought about it. And yeah, I think I'm ready. I still have moments when I question God. He could have stopped her."

"No one blames you for that. I imagine we could

all put together a list of things we question God over. Why someone we loved died in a car accident or why someone had to die young. And the only answer is that sin entered the world and we are allowed free will. We make choices that change lives."

Wyatt fought a real strong urge to say something about this move and if it was really what God wanted or was he giving Pastor Waters freedom to choose, right or wrong. But he knew that Robert Waters was a praying man. He didn't make hasty decisions. He followed what he felt God wanted for him.

He didn't want this man to leave. But maybe it really had been God's plan to have Pastor Waters in Dawson for this season to do the things he needed to do here before moving somewhere else where God had another plan.

"This isn't going to be an easy move for us." Pastor Waters sighed at the end of the sentence and shook his head. "Rachel loves Dawson. She loves taking care of your girls."

"They love her, too."

Pastor Waters glanced his way and smiled. "I guess you've asked her to consider staying?"

"I have, but she won't."

"No, I didn't figure she would."

Family issues, everyone had them. For Wyatt it

was all about making his girls his first priority. His parents had never made that a rule. For his parents, life had been about parties and what made them happy. Their two boys were pictures they showed when they wanted to brag about something other than money or the land they owned.

He'd never be his parents. He ran the family business from a distance and his girls came first. Especially now.

Across the lawn Violet and Rachel were cleaning up the leftover party favors, the empty cups and paper plates that were blowing off the picnic table. They talked in quiet whispers like two old friends.

That scene made him a little itchy on the inside, so he turned to search for his girls. They were swinging, feet dangling and party crowns still on their heads. Molly had the biggest crown, the queen crown. And each girl had pink satin ballerina slippers.

He'd never seen so much pink in one place.

"I think I'll go check on my girls." He pushed himself out of the chair, wincing a little at the catch in his ribs and the pull across his lower back. He'd never been so glad to see a horse go as he had been to watch that buckskin loaded into the trailer yesterday afternoon.

He would have kept the animal around if Ryder

had been able to take over training for a week or two. But they both had different priorities now.

"Molly, did you have a good birthday?" He stood behind his daughters, pushing one and then the other.

"The bestest one ever." Molly looked back at him, smiling big.

His gaze traveled the short distance to Rachel Waters. The bestest ever. He decided to feel a little angry with her and with God because she was going to leave them empty again.

Last night he'd had to tell the girls. They'd both cried and Molly had begged him to make Rachel stay. She wouldn't, he'd explained. She had responsibilities. Molly asked him what that word meant. He'd had to find a way to explain it to a four-year-old.

Things that matter. Responsibility is the things that we have to do because they matter, they come first. Family, the farm, a job. Those were responsibilities. Molly wanted to be Rachel's responsibility.

The things that come first.

Rachel laughed, the sound carrying. He tried to picture this yard, this house and their lives with her gone.

They'd be empty again.

He gave Kat an easy push. No, they wouldn't

be empty. They would still have each other. And they'd have something else. They had the ability to move on and to laugh.

Two weeks after Molly's party, Rachel walked through a ranch house on the outskirts of Tulsa, just a few blocks from her dad's new church. The church was larger than any he'd ever pastored. The benefits were clearly the best. It was something wonderful for her parents. It meant having a real retirement and security.

It meant great medical care.

It meant Rachel moving into a small bedroom with purple carpet and green walls. Obviously a teenager had been here. Rachel felt a little dizzy, standing in the center of that room.

"It's a nice little house." Her mother stood at the window looking out at the tiny little yard. Rachel didn't want to look. She knew what she'd see outside that window. She'd had views like this before.

She would see other houses, back to back, side to side. She would see privacy fences and manicured shrubs. There would be a patio and eventually patio furniture. Her dog would go on a leash and they'd take walks around the neighborhood. They would talk to strangers who would possibly become friends.

They would adjust. They always did.

And she would live this life until? Until her parents no longer needed her. She smiled at her mom, who hadn't looked this happy in a long time. The idea of a big church with a large staff had taken a burden off her mother.

Gloria Waters wouldn't feel guilty, as if she was letting her husband or his congregation down because she couldn't take a more active role in the ministry. Rachel wanted to tell her mother that they had her, she took that burden. She carried that weight for them.

Cynthia, her sister, had called that morning as they drove into Tulsa. She had given Rachel a lecture about being a martyr because she didn't want to take chances in life. It was easy to stay with their parents, to not get involved in real life.

Rachel had ended the conversation with a blunt "Goodbye."

It was easy for Cynthia. Life had always been easy for the pretty blonde with the stick figure and the outgoing personality. Cynthia had married her college sweetheart. She'd never been rejected.

Her dad stuck his head around the corner. "Nice room."

Rachel smiled. "Love the colors."

"I thought you would." He stepped into the room. "You can paint if you want."

"I know." She smiled, pretending to love the idea of painting another room.

She would be thirty in a few months. Thirty and living with her parents. What did people think? Did they think she was somehow defective? Did they get that she wanted to be here to help?

"Let's take a walk around the neighborhood." Rachel's dad reached for her hand. "I think there's a pool down the block."

"Dad, I'm not fifteen."

He laughed a little. "Yeah, I know. But swimming is great exercise. You can jog one day and swim the next."

She remembered this from her teen years. Her parents always broke the news about moving by telling them how great the new place would be. Eventually Rachel stopped caring. She stopped seeing the moves as an adventure. It became about having to learn a new school, make new friends and reinvent herself each time.

She no longer reinvented.

But she did go for a walk with her dad. He held Wolfgang's leash and they took their time, letting the dog sniff all of the new scents.

"Rachel, have you prayed about this move?"

"What do you mean?"

He stopped while the dog took particular interest in a sign post. "I mean, have you prayed for yourself? Is this move what you're supposed to do?"

"Dad, we're here. I'm here."

Her dad continued to walk and she stayed next to him, whistling to get the dog's attention when it appeared a little too interested in a neighbor's cat. That wouldn't be a good way to start this new life.

"Rachel, I want you to make a decision based on what *you* want."

"What I want is to be here helping you and Mom."

"I'm not sure about that. I kind of wonder if you aren't sacrificing your own happiness because of some sense of duty to your mother and me."

"You've been talking to Cynthia." Rachel took Wolfgang's leash because she needed to control something. Her life was obviously out of the question.

"I talked to Rob and Cynthia. They're both concerned that you're giving up what you want because you feel as if we need you."

"That's nice of them." The brother and sister who visited once a year suddenly knew what was best for her and for their parents.

The thought was unfair, but at the moment she didn't feel like being fair.

"Rachel, I'm about to do something I should

have done a long time ago. I'm pushing you from the nest."

"Pushing me?"

She wasn't stupid, but seriously, where had this come from?

"Rachel, years ago God called me to this ministry. He called me. He called your mother with me. We had children. Now our children are grown and it is time for you, my daughter, to find your own place. Your mother and I can take care of ourselves. We took care of you. We really are able to handle life."

"But when Mom is sick…"

He smiled and she felt ten again. "Rachel, I'm her husband. I can take care of her. Go and live your life, make your own choices. When I took this position I knew it was right for me, right for your mother. I think you have to pray about the right place for you."

"Here." She held tight to the leash and fought tears that burned her eyes.

"If that's what God's plan is, fine. With us, in Tulsa, or back in Dawson, it doesn't matter as long as you know it's the right place for you." He kissed her cheek. "Go do something for yourself, Rachel. Eat chocolate, find something you love. Or *someone* you love. Stop using us as an excuse to avoid your own life."

"Ouch."

He laughed a little. "Sorry, but the truth can hurt. You pray and if, after you pray, you honestly feel like it is God's will for you to move here, then I'll accept that."

"I'm starting to get a very big hint." The hint that her parents would like to be alone.

"I thought you might."

Right, so where did that leave her?

Wyatt backed the trailer up to the corral gate, watching the side mirrors as he eased back. He stopped when the open gate hit the back of the trailer. Perfect.

The dog that had followed next to his truck started to bark. Wyatt turned off the truck and watched Rachel's car easing up the drive. He let out a shallow breath, still not taking deep breaths because his ribs wouldn't give that much. He stepped out of the truck and waited for her to get out of her car.

He hadn't expected her today. For the last week she'd been packing, loading boxes and getting the church staff ready to take over her many jobs. They didn't have a new pastor, not yet. Wyatt and a few other men had prayed about the decision. For now they'd take turns preaching, just until they could find the right man.

The dog left his side and ran to hers, tail wagging.

Rachel reached to pet the animal. It followed her back to him. He glanced toward the house. Violet was inside with the girls. She'd been interviewing housekeepers. So far he and the girls hadn't liked any of the candidates.

"I didn't expect to see you today."

She shrugged one shoulder and didn't look directly at him. Her brown hair blew around her face and her expression seemed a little lost to him.

"I hadn't expected to stop. I missed the girls and wanted to give them something I bought in Tulsa."

"They've missed you, too." He almost included himself, but he wasn't going there.

What did he miss? Her pancakes, coffee that didn't taste bitter, or music blasting as she cleaned?

"Do you mind if I go in and see them?"

"No, go ahead. I have to load some calves that we've sold." The reason he'd backed the trailer up to the corral. The bawling calves were huddled in the far corner of the corral.

"I could help you."

"I can get it." He tried not to move like someone who needed help. She laughed at his attempt.

"Let me help. I'll miss this." The faraway look

returned. "We're moving into a neighborhood where our view is of the neighbor's back door."

"I've lived in those neighborhoods. It works for a lot of people. I guess it's a good thing we're all different."

"Yeah. So I can help?"

He pointed her to the gate. "I'll head them this way. You make sure they don't squeeze through there."

She nodded and headed for the spot he pointed to. She wasn't country at all, just wanted to be. That was okay with him. He enjoyed watching her standing there in her denim shorts, a T-shirt and sandals. Not exactly a picture of a cowgirl, but he didn't really know what a cowgirl was supposed to look like. He'd seen a few in his time that looked like anything but.

The calves moved away from him. His dog circled, keeping them together and moving toward the trailer. One angus steer tried to break from the group, the dog brought him back, nipping quick at the steer's hooves.

Ahead of him, Rachel stood next to the gate, her hand shading her eyes as the sun hit. He didn't smile, couldn't. He was picturing her in that house surrounded by neighbors.

The calves ran through the opening into the back of the trailer. He swung the trailer door, swinging the latch in place. The calves moved to the back of the trailer.

Wyatt slid through the gate. Rachel moved out of his way.

"You don't have to go."

Her eyes widened and she stared, waiting. He didn't know what to say other than what he'd said. He lifted a hand and rested it on the side of the trailer.

"I kind of do have to go. I don't have a home here. My parents are moving."

"Rachel, the girls don't want any other nanny. They already miss you and you're not gone."

"Of course, I know they'll miss me. I'll miss them, too. But I feel like I need to be close to my parents. If my mom gets sick, I need to be there."

"It isn't that far. What is it, just under two hours to their new church?"

"Something like that. But if she's sick, she needs daily help, not a visit."

"Right, you're right." He let it go because he did understand her loyalty to her parents. He got it.

"I'm going to go see the girls. I want them to know that I'll visit."

He smiled and tipped his hat. "Yeah, visits are good. I have to get these steers on down the road."

She turned and walked away. He watched her walk through the back door of his house and then he climbed in the truck and cranked the engine. He eased forward, watching in the rearview mirror as the corral gate swung shut. The trailer shifted as the cattle shifted.

In the house Rachel was telling his girls goodbye. Why did he have the sudden urge to hit something? It combined with a pretty nasty urge to turn the truck and stock trailer around.

And do what? Beg Rachel to stay? What would he tell her? He could tell her that his girls were happier with her in their lives. *He* was happier.

After that, what then? He would have her in their home as a housekeeper and nanny. She would cook for them, clean their house and hug the girls. He'd still have to deal with moving on.

Last night he'd pulled out photo albums. He'd glanced through pictures of Wendy in college. They were young and in love. Crazy in love.

He rode bulls and roped steers. She spent weekends working at a homeless shelter. They'd picked youth ministry together. After college they'd gotten married.

The pictures stayed happy for a few years, until after Molly's birth. That was when the story of their lives changed. He'd looked at those pictures and tried to figure out what he could have done.

But he couldn't change things. He couldn't undo them now. What he had was a future with his two little girls and memories of their mother. Someday he'd share the good memories.

None of that fixed the situation right now. Rachel was going to leave and Violet was hiring a new housekeeper. She'd talked about a lady named Thelda Matheson. He hoped she wore joint cream.

Chapter Seventeen

Rachel stood in the green-and-purple bedroom staring out a window without a view and knowing this was all wrong. She was in the wrong place, in the wrong life. It felt like wearing someone else's shoes.

Her parents were drinking coffee in the new kitchen, sitting in front of patio doors at a table they'd had for years. Same table, same parents, different kitchen. Same life. Their life.

She joined them at that table. They looked up, not asking questions. She got up to pour herself a cup of coffee and then she joined them again.

"You're right, this isn't my place anymore."

"What does that mean?" Her mom put her cup down and glanced at Rachel's dad. The two seemed to always know everything she was about to tell them.

When she had been sixteen and rebellious,

nothing ever seemed to surprise them. They always seemed to know what trouble she'd gotten herself into.

"I left my ministry." Rachel wiped at tears that were rolling down her cheeks. "I left my home."

"Dawson?" Her dad smiled, as if he'd planned it himself.

"Yes, Dawson. The teen girls. My Sunday school class. Molly and Kat. I left it all because I thought you needed me here. But God called you to make this move, not me. It's just that I'm stubborn or afraid, I'm not sure which."

"And you thought I needed you." Gloria patted her hand. "Honey, I will always need you, but I'm really okay."

"I know you are. Maybe I wasn't. Maybe I've needed you."

"I think we just got into the bad habit of letting you take care of us." Her mom smiled. "What do you plan on doing?"

"I think I'm going to call Etta and see if I can still take her up on the offer to stay at her house. I'll call the church and ask if I can keep working with the kids."

"It feels good, doesn't it?" Her dad grinned big.

"Yeah, it kind of does feel good. This is right, Dad."

"I think I tried to tell you that the other day. Time to fly, Rachel. Go find your future."

She carried her still-full cup to the sink. "I think I'm going to start packing."

The one thing she wouldn't do was make this move about Wyatt. He'd hired a new housekeeper. The girls needed to get settled with the person he'd found. Rachel needed to make sure she was where God wanted her, not jump back into what felt comfortable and easy.

She needed to wait because she didn't want a broken heart her first day back in her new life.

Wyatt drove past the parsonage a few days after Rachel's last visit. It was empty. He let out a sigh and kept on going. She was gone and Mrs. Matheson had taken her place. He didn't like the lady. No reason, he just didn't like her. He didn't like her sensible shoes or the smell of eucalyptus that hovered over her as she moved through the house.

Kat and Molly weren't crazy about her either.

He pulled up the drive and parked inside the garage. Violet was still at the house. She assured him she would be leaving in the morning. They'd be fine without her.

Of course they would. He walked out of the garage and across the yard to the barn. The stallion he'd bought from the Fosters whinnied from the small corral at the side of the barn. Wyatt walked up to the fence and the big bay, his dark red coat gleaming, trotted up for a treat. Wyatt pulled an apple snack out of his pocket and the horse sucked it up, barely grazing his hands.

The back door banged shut. He turned. It was Violet. She walked toward him, her high heels sinking in the yard that was still soggy from last night's rain. He wondered if she would ever try to fit into these surroundings. He doubted it.

"Did you see Rachel before she left?" Violet stood next to him, holding her hand out to the horse but withdrawing it before the horse made contact.

"No, I didn't see her. I think they left last night."

"Right." Violet stepped back because the horse stuck his nose out to her.

"What is it you want to say, Violet?"

She smiled up at him. "Don't let her go."

"What does that mean? I offered her the job, she turned it down. How can I change that?" He really wanted to walk away from this conversation. "I've hired someone. Remember?"

"Don't be ridiculous, I'm not talking about hiring her as a housekeeper. I'm talking about what you seem to be ignoring or avoiding. You love her. It's obvious she loves you. Why in the world are you letting her go?"

The mother of his wife, pushing him to—what?

"Violet, this isn't the conversation I want to have with you."

"No, I'm sure it isn't. But I think I'm the best person to tell you that Wendy would want you to move on. She'd want it to be with someone like Rachel, someone who loves you and your girls. This kind of love doesn't happen often. For most people it happens once. You're blessed to have it happen twice. Don't let this get away."

"It's too soon." He pushed his hat down on his head, tipping the brim to shade his eyes.

"Who says?"

"I say." He backed away from the fence, from the horse, from Violet. "I say it's too soon."

"You can't control that. You're trying to hold on to her memory and the love you shared. I get that. But you can't say it's too soon. Not if the right person has entered your life and you're on the verge of losing her. If you haven't already lost her."

"I have to go for a drive."

"Fine, go for a drive. But if I was you, I'd spend time praying about this. I don't believe in chance, Wyatt Johnson. It was no accident that she was here, in your life and in the lives of your daughters."

"Violet, let it go."

She drew in her lips and shook her head. "Wyatt, you're stubborn."

He walked away, back to his truck, back to a few minutes alone. As he drove down the drive, he thought back to her words. He remembered telling Rachel that he wasn't ready.

He hadn't planned on ever being ready.

And Rachel had made a choice. He'd asked her to stay and she'd made the decision to go.

Because he hadn't asked her to stay for him. He called himself every kind of fool because he knew he'd asked the wrong question.

Fly, little bird, fly. Rachel smiled as the wind whipped through her hair. The radio blasted Sara Evans and she sang along to a song about suds being left in the bucket and clothes left hanging on the line.

Rachel Waters was finally leaving home. After the conversation with her parents a few days ago, she'd taken time to figure out exactly what she wanted. She knew it wasn't Tulsa. As much as she loved the city, she didn't want to live there.

And it had been pretty obvious her parents didn't need her. It had been more obvious that maybe they were a little relieved to hear that she planned on moving out.

She'd watched them together, watched her mom

and dad taking care of each other, unpacking, planning. She'd watched herself on the outside of their circle, trying to be helpful, trying to take care of them. And all along they could take care of themselves.

She'd stopped taking risks. A long time ago she'd decided safe was good. Well, today was a new day. Today included giving in a little, maybe even giving in to temptation.

So on the way out of Tulsa she'd gone through a drive-through for a frozen coffee drink full of calories and a cookie laden down with chocolate chips. Take that, thighs.

Rachel Waters was done controlling her life. She planned on finding her path, her future, her today. With God in control.

Today. No more waiting for tomorrow. No more fear of taking risks.

She had called Etta who'd been overjoyed with the idea of Rachel staying with her for a while, helping on the farm and with her business. Vera had answered the next call and agreed to give her a few lunch shifts during the week.

Rachel cruised through Dawson, slow, taking it all in. Home. She smiled, loving that word. The one place she had loved more than any other and now it was her home. Her choice. She had a place to go and a nice savings account. It felt good. It felt better than good.

It felt pretty close to perfect until she drove past Wyatt's and saw the girls on the swing. It shouldn't hurt, that he'd offered her a job. But it did. He wanted her in their lives, but only as the person who cooked meals, gave hugs and went home at the end of every day.

She wanted more than that.

The old convictions were still strong, the belief that God would bring the right person into her life. As she got older she wondered if maybe that wasn't His plan. Not everyone had the same destiny. There was a point in time when a person just accepted what his or her life was and made peace with it.

Etta's house was a welcome sight. The big, yellow Victorian glowed in the setting sun. Rachel pulled up the drive and parked. When she walked around the corner of the house, Etta met her on the sidewalk.

"Well, aren't you a sight for sore eyes." Etta grabbed her in a tight hug.

"It's only been a few days."

"Longest days of my life, wondering if you'd get it right."

Rachel laughed and hugged Etta back. "I got it right."

Etta slid an arm around Rachel's waist and they walked up the steps to the porch. "At least partially right."

"How much more right do I need to be?"

Etta turned at the sound of a car coming down the road. No, it was a truck. Rachel's heart froze in place, refusing to pick up where it left off. She took a deep breath and her heart did the same.

"Hmm, someone else must be trying to get it right."

"No, Etta." Rachel refused to watch the truck drive on by.

"Oh, you kids. I tell you what, in the last year, I've had it up to my neck with silly young couples who take forever to get it right. It was simpler in my day. The man knew what he wanted and he went after it. The woman knew it was the right thing to do and she stopped running. Happy ever after."

Rachel wanted to laugh but she couldn't. The truck didn't go on down the road, it pulled into Etta's drive.

Etta chuckled a little. "Don't run, Rachel. I'm going inside and you let yourself get caught."

"I have a job. I'm going to work for you. He found someone else to watch the girls."

Etta had walked inside. The screen door closed behind her.

"Oh, honey, you are clueless."

Rachel stood on the porch waiting for Wyatt to get out of the truck and join her. He walked a little easier than he had the previous week. It hadn't been that long, she reminded herself. But honestly, the last week had felt like a lifetime.

"So this is where you went to." He walked up the steps. He took off his hat and held it in front of him, raising one hand and running it through dark hair flattened to his head.

She'd been right about him, he was heartache and she didn't need heartache, not even if it came in a package with lean, suntanned cheeks and a smile that nearly became a caress.

"I came back." She eased the words out.

"I know. I've been in Tulsa."

"What? Why?"

"To talk to your dad."

"Oh."

"And to see you." He stepped closer. His dark eyes held hers captive.

"Really?" Her heart took a hopeful leap forward but she pulled it back, reined it in. Maybe the new housekeeper hadn't worked out.

"Yeah, really." His smile was sweet, it melted in his eyes and melted her heart. Wasn't that the same heart she was trying to keep under control?

For some reason it wasn't working, that control thing.

"How are the girls?"

He reached for her hands. "The girls miss you."

"I miss them, too."

He tossed his hat on a nearby chair. "I miss you, too."

"I see."

"No, you don't. Rachel, I got up this morning and walked around a house that has never felt more empty. I realized what was missing. You." He teased her with another one of those smiles. "I realized I asked you the wrong question."

She didn't know what to say.

"You are the thing missing from our lives. From *my* life. I went to Tulsa because I wanted to see you. I wanted to tell you that I don't want you in our lives as a housekeeper or a nanny."

Her heart wouldn't let go of hope. It wouldn't stop its crazy beat inside her chest. She couldn't move, couldn't breathe.

"Rachel, I want you in our lives because we love you. I love you."

"You do?" She loved him, too, but she was afraid to say the words, afraid to believe this moment was happening.

He grinned and brushed a hand across her cheek.

"I do. While I was in Tulsa, I asked your dad to do me a favor."

"What's that?" Was that her heart melting, pooling up inside her?

"I asked him if he would do the honor of officiating at a wedding."

"Oh."

"I told him I'd like to date his daughter for a few months." He pulled her close, touching his lips to hers, sweet, seductive and then gone. "And I asked him if he would walk you down the aisle and then step behind the pulpit and marry us."

"Wyatt." She whispered the word close to his ear and he turned, brushing his cheek against hers.

"So now I need to ask you, Rachel Waters, if you'll be the wife of one very hard-headed cowboy. This isn't about being ready to move on. This is about being ready to love you for the rest of my life."

Rachel closed her eyes, replaying his words, the words she'd been waiting for, wanting to hear. She'd dreamed of those words and how it would feel at this moment. And now she knew. She knew that shivers would tingle up her arms and down her spine. She knew that her heart would twirl inside her chest.

She now knew that he would lean and his hands

would cup her cheeks as he dropped the sweetest kiss on her lips.

But in her dreams it had never been this wonderful.

"Rachel, will you marry me?" Wyatt whispered the proposal again after kissing her long and easy.

She nodded and tears pooled and slid down her cheeks.

"Of course I'll marry you."

Wyatt held his breath as she said the words he'd been waiting to hear and then he released his hand from hers and fished the ring out of his shirt pocket.

"I was hoping you might say yes." He grinned, his face a little warm. "So I stopped at a jewelry store on the way home and told them I needed the most beautiful diamond for the most beautiful bride."

She stood in front of him, sweeter than cherry soda on a hot summer day and everything he wanted in life. He reached for her hand and slid the ring onto her finger. The diamond glinted, winking the promise of forever.

"I love you," he whispered.

He held her close, thankful to have her in his

arms again. She felt good there, in his arms. She felt right. This felt right.

This was something only a fool would let go of. He wasn't a fool. He might be a hard-headed cowboy, but he knew what he wanted and he knew when to hold on to it.

She moved her hands to his shoulders and then to the back of his neck as he captured her lips in a kiss that promised forever.

"I love you, too." She whispered close to his ear and he held her tight.

No way would he ever let her go.

Epilogue

Wyatt walked out of the barn and saw his wife
and kids in the backyard. Ryder stood behind him.
The two of them had been working cattle all day,
giving immunizations and taking care of other
details that had to be dealt with. Little bull calves
were now steers. Ears were tagged.

The two of them were dirty and pretty close to
disgusting.

Ryder slapped his back. "Brother, that's a nice
little family you've got."

Wyatt smiled and he couldn't agree more. But
he wasn't going to give Ryder room to gloat. He
knew where Ryder was going with this conversation. Wyatt counted to three and waited for it.

On cue Ryder spoke, a big smile on his face.
"Wasn't it just a couple of years ago that I said
something about needing a boy in our family to
protect all of these girls?"

Wyatt continued to ignore his little brother. Listen to Ryder, or watch his family playing together in the backyard. He picked ignoring the pest at his side. Even if he was right.

"Yep, that's one cute little baby boy you've got." Ryder, loose limbed and way too sure of himself, took off across the yard. Andie had the twins in a big playpen, keeping the "little fillies" as Ryder called his girls, corralled.

Wyatt smiled when Rachel turned to find him. She was more beautiful today than she'd been on their wedding day. That day, dressed in a cream gown and walking down the aisle with her dad, that had been a day.

But today, with their little boy tucked safe in the pouch that hung around her neck, today she glowed. Today, just looking at her knocked him on his can.

He choked up a little, thinking about Rowdy's birth. He had feared losing Rachel. He'd been afraid she'd slip away.

Now those thoughts were pushed aside. He had a wife, two beautiful daughters and one handsome little guy.

"Are you going to come and push your daughters?" Rachel called out, bringing him back to earth.

"On my way." He hurried across the lawn. When

he got there he kissed her first, holding her close for a minute, loose in his arms. And then he kissed the dark head of his little boy.

God had brought her to Dawson and then brought him home. Good planning, God. He smiled as he pushed Molly high and gave Kat a lighter push.

Good planning.

* * * * *

Dear Reader,

Welcome back to my favorite fictional small town; Dawson, Oklahoma. I love Oklahoma. I've never lived there, but if I had to move, that's the direction I'd head. Oklahoma has history, horses, ranches… and let's not forget: cowboys.

I hope you enjoy Rachel and Wyatt's story. When Wyatt Johnson first arrived back in Dawson, I knew that his story had to be told. It is a story about healing and moving past our pain.

It is also about trusting God with where we are in our lives.

It was obvious that Wyatt would need a woman who could handle his pain and stand up to him when he was hard-headed. Enter pastor's daughter Rachel Waters. As you read Rachel and Wyatt's story, I hope it touches your life. And if you're dealing with your own pain, I pray that God heals your heart.

Brenda Minton

QUESTIONS FOR DISCUSSION

1. Without knowing Ryder and Wyatt's phone conversation, Rachel assumes it is about her, and about Wyatt not wanting someone like herself pushed off on him. Why would that be her first assumption?

2. Wyatt is getting over his wife's suicide. How does his faith come into play?

3. How effectively is Wyatt dealing with grief and raising his daughters?

4. How does Rachel's childhood play into the person she has become and why?

5. Wyatt has a difficult time leaving his girls. Is his protectiveness about faith or lack of faith, or not about faith at all?

6. How does Rachel's childhood weight issues affect her as an adult?

7. Wyatt realizes he has gone through stages of grief. Do you believe he moved forward a step, and if so, when?

8. Rachel and Wyatt are like most of us, drawn to one another and fighting the attraction, including the chemistry that pulls them together. Do you believe they made wise choices in their relationship, and how?

9. Rachel steps further into Wyatt's life by taking the job with his children. How will this change their relationship, or will it?

10. When do you think Rachel falls in love with Wyatt?

11. What reasons does Rachel have for wanting to stay with her parents? Are those real reasons or excuses, or maybe both?

12. Wyatt is willing to let Rachel go because of his own fears. What do you think those fears are, and how does he overcome them?

13. Rachel's parents allowed her to stay at home with them all these years. What helped them to see that it was time for her to move on with her own life and make choices that are right for her?

14. When Rachel finally chooses her own path, how do faith and her own desires play into the decision?

LARGER-PRINT BOOKS!

**GET 2 FREE
LARGER-PRINT NOVELS
PLUS 2 FREE
MYSTERY GIFTS**

Larger-print novels are now available...

YES! Please send me 2 FREE LARGER-PRINT Love Inspired® novels and my 2 FREE mystery gifts (gifts are worth about $10). After receiving them, if I don't wish to receive any more books, I can return the shipping statement marked "cancel". If I don't cancel, I will receive 6 brand-new novels every month and be billed just $4.74 per book in the U.S. or $5.24 per book in Canada. That's a saving of over 20% off the cover price. It's quite a bargain! Shipping and handling is just 50¢ per book.* I understand that accepting the 2 free books and gifts places me under no obligation to buy anything. I can always return a shipment and cancel at any time. Even if I never buy another book, the two free books and gifts are mine to keep forever.

122/322 IDN E7QP

Name _____ (PLEASE PRINT) _____

Address _____ Apt. # _____

City _____ State/Prov. _____ Zip/Postal Code _____

Signature (if under 18, a parent or guardian must sign) _____

Mail to **Steeple Hill Reader Service:**
IN U.S.A.: P.O. Box 1867, Buffalo, NY 14240-1867
IN CANADA: P.O. Box 609, Fort Erie, Ontario L2A 5X3

Not valid to current subscribers to Love Inspired Larger-Print books.

**Are you a current subscriber to Love Inspired books
and want to receive the larger-print edition?
Call 1-800-873-8635 or visit www.morefreebooks.com.**

* Terms and prices subject to change without notice. Prices do not include applicable taxes. Sales tax applicable in N.Y. Canadian residents will be charged applicable provincial taxes and GST. Offer not valid in Quebec. This offer is limited to one order per household. All orders subject to approval. Credit or debit balances in a customer's account(s) may be offset by any other outstanding balance owed by or to the customer. Please allow 4 to 6 weeks for delivery. Offer available while quantities last.

Your Privacy: Steeple Hill Books is committed to protecting your privacy. Our Privacy Policy is available online at www.SteepleHill.com or upon request from the Reader Service. From time to time we make our lists of customers available to reputable third parties who may have a product or service of interest to you. If you would prefer we not share your name and address, please check here. ☐

Help us get it right—We strive for accurate, respectful and relevant communications. To clarify or modify your communication preferences, visit us at www.ReaderService.com/consumerschoice.

LILP10R

Love Inspired®
SUSPENSE
RIVETING INSPIRATIONAL ROMANCE

Watch for our new series of
edge-of-your-seat suspense novels.
These contemporary tales
of intrigue and romance
feature Christian characters
facing challenges to their faith...
and their lives!

NOW AVAILABLE IN REGULAR & LARGER-PRINT FORMATS

Steeple
Hill®

Visit:
www.SteepleHill.com

LISUSDIR10

ReaderService.com

You can now manage your account online!

- Review your order history
- Manage your payments
- Update your address

We've redesigned the Reader Service website just for you.

Now you can:

- Read excerpts
- Respond to mailings and special monthly offers
- Learn about new series available to you

Visit us today:

www.ReaderService.com

RS10